HER V

Noa

**HER WILD BODY**
**Noa Raveh**

Copyright © 2025 Noa Raveh

All rights reserved; no parts of this book may be reproduced or transmitted in any form or by any means, electronic or mechanical, including photocopying, recording, taping, or by any information retrieval system, without the permission, in writing, of the author.

Translation from Hebrew: Sharon Hollombe
Editing: Nancy Alroy

Contact: info@malka-press.com

ISBN 9798312028638

# HER *Wild* BODY

*A steamy, later-in-life, sapphic romance*

**NOA RAVEH**

# Contents

Esther - 2021 .................................................................. 9

**First Portal:** Noga - 2017 .............................................. 13

**Second Portal:** Mowgli - 2020 ...................................... 77

**Third Portal:** Shira, for a Moment - 2020 ................... 127

**Fourth Portal:** Tammy Gil - 2021 ................................ 139

**Fifth Portal:** Esther Lionheart - 2021 ......................... 169

Esther - 2023 ................................................................ 275

*To the woman with the lion in her belly, Miriam.*

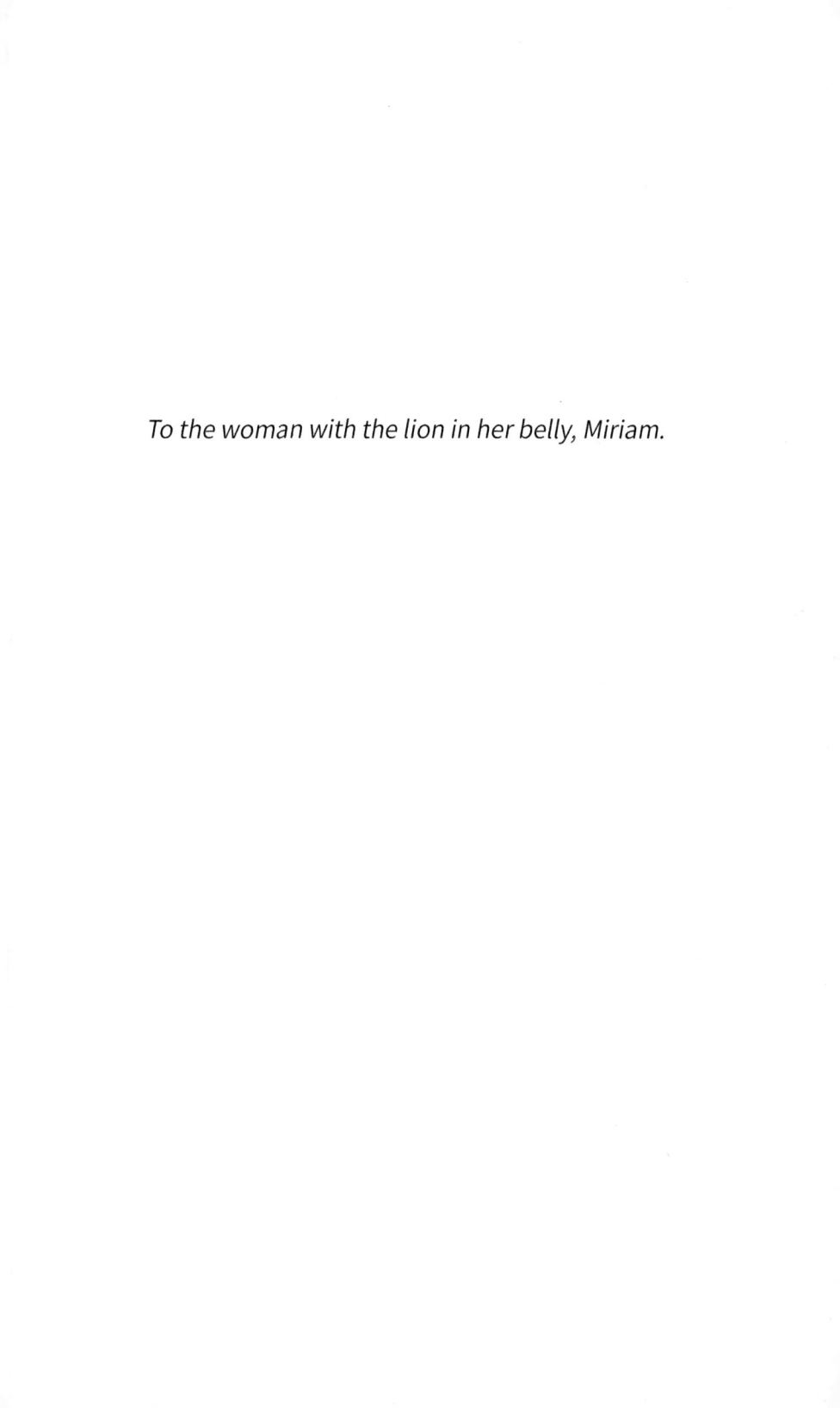

**ESTHER
2021**

# It's Not Just the Earth That's Shaking

You touch me and I get chills from the nape of my neck to the soles of my feet. A softness spreads within me, hot and wide like the summer. You enter me and fuck me hard, painting the walls of my soul from within. You quietly set up a house of prayer for us between dark blue sheets embroidered with gold.

We splash around in sweat, whiskey and pussy. Breathing each other in and out. Desire materializes through us and becomes, for a few hours, woman's flesh.

How you know me, how you hear all the secrets I've buried. I celebrate your sure movement inside me, trusting your strong hands and your eyes that know how to change colors.

You put a kaffiyeh and a tallit together, dipping them in color, testing if they can breathe as one. They called you a terrorist artist and yet you are a peacemaker. The terror they are most afraid of is love. And the wolf shall dwell with the lamb, woman with woman.

We'll lick pussy here until we vanquish the war, the sirens, the guardians of all walls. We sigh and moan peace and love on your bed, in our mouths, between the palms of our hands. Sacred becomes us. We become sacred.

I shed hairs, leaving them for you in every corner of the house, like strings asking to tie you to me. You anoint me with rose water, agua de flores seeping into my neck and belly. When I leave, I still carry your scent, stealing back to you in the hours that follow. My body echoes you, my nostrils remind my brain of the storms we created in your bed, all the waves we rode together.

"What are you doing to my sense of smell?" I ask.

"It's the scent and the spirit," you answer.

You and your words, you and your colors. Paint inside a church, you tell me? Inside a woman, you inhale and exhale here.

When I leave and the door closes behind me, I already know. There is no other woman, there never was. You are everything. You've penetrated the crispiest layers, where every movement matters. You are both my destination and my place of origin. I knew, you are where time begins.

First Portal

**NOGA**
2017

# The Way it Works

I'm hot. It's hot inside me. My heart bursts, my hips dance, my stomach storms. We inhale, we exhale, we drip with grace. She bites my arm. "Harder," I beg, mark me, imprint yourself on me. Her vagina tightens around my hand like a fierce embrace, and I feel her orgasm climbing from her clitoris to her navel, to her chest, to her windpipe. I'm so aroused, I ascend with her—a star-bursting orgasm rocks her and shatters against my hand. We embrace, calm down, breathe together, and tears well up in my throat.

The clock chimes at midnight for the two Cinderellas who must return home. Once a week, we meet at a friend's apartment, halfway between her house and mine. Between her husband and mine. Between her children and mine. Once a week, I try to drink her in, to swallow her whole. Just once, I want to be satiated, but always, always, that clock rings—its synthetic, indifferent chimes showing no mercy. I'm never fully satisfied.

We rise. Dress and kiss. Make the bed, fluff the pillows, and kiss. Turn off the air conditioning and lights, and kiss. By one in the morning, we manage to part. We tear ourselves from each other, each to her own car. The warmth of her body still heats me against the night's chill. Her scent lingers deep in my nostrils—a parting gift. A brilliant biological trick easing the transition back to the world without her.

I drive home slowly. Lights, cars, my eyes narrowed from exhaustion, my body regulating its breath. The smell of pussy and her shampoo fill the car. I sniff my right hand like a junky craving her fix.

Another half hour and I'll touch down but, until then, I allow myself to float a bit longer. To imagine my red polish against her pale skin. To taste her on my lips. Her witch-fairy-sorceress hands in my vagina, in the deepest chambers of my heart.

I enter the house silently. Everyone is asleep except the dog who greets me. He's always overjoyed when I return, completely out of sync with the hour and circumstances. Quietly, I prepare for bed. Wash my hands with soap. Brush my teeth. Don't shower. I need her scent to linger on me a while longer. I slip into bed noiselessly. His breathing is steady, filling the space. He turns in his sleep to embrace me, and I drift off in his strong arms.

Morning erupts with the commotion of children. Sandwiches. Shoelaces. Don't forget the basketball and the math notebook. I didn't get enough sleep but I'm wide awake. "How was it?" he asks over the children's heads as they eat cornflakes. "Amazing," I answer. That's all he asks. That's all I tell.

We made an agreement. "Love her," he said, "do what you want but don't share with me, I don't want to know the details."

This works perfectly because I have no desire to share with him. She is the autonomy in my life's landscape. A small, private island, sweet and delicious and rare in its beauty. Once a week, freedom to love as we wish. Beyond that, I'm his. Beyond that, she's with him.

He's my man. I looked into his eyes when I gave birth, when life came. He argues with me and hurts me. He's my earth and my blood. The anchor and the respectability. She's my girlfriend, my beloved. She's the quietest, deepest secret. When we meet, she silences ancient demons within me. With airy gentleness she touches, and all my cells soften. She's my Venus rising from the sea, she is my heart's sun.

Usually, it's good. Most times I manage to maneuver between everything and everyone. I live with an internal hourglass that flips each week, but this heart of mine doesn't understand time and space and sometimes I want her so much. Sometimes her absence, the intense void, catches me like a wooden stick sideways in my throat and I drown in desperate, unbearable longing. I'm willing to give so much for one whiff of her neck, for one finger on her bare skin.

Forced separation by choice, it's the strange concept we've created that protects us from falling apart, from dismantling everything we've built and those who depend on us.

My chest burns with missing you, I write to her. I promised myself I wouldn't do that. That I wouldn't burden her with my pinched heart. That I wouldn't hang on her with this thick, heavy neediness. And yet here I am, breaking my promises.

I rub the mark she left on my arm. I want to roar and bite and go wild against the distance between us, but I collect myself. Fold laundry into neat piles in the living room. Chop the salad finely, the way they like it, with avocado on the side. Help with long division. Divide myself into more and more pieces, enough for everyone.

# My Non-Biological Sister

It's Wednesday at 6pm and we each head our separate ways. "Enjoy," she says to me. "It's already cunt o' clock." Wednesday at 6pm, now dubbed 'cunt o' clock' is when Dana heads out to visit her lover, a Rastafarian who lives in a caravan at the edge of a forest in the Western Galilee, while I go to my beautiful beloved. That's how it is with sisters. We're in sync. We even menstruate together, despite living a two-hour drive apart.

Dana is my best friend, my non-biological sister. We met at a sacred song circle, one of those ceremonial gatherings where people sing and play music together. We were instantly drawn to each other. She has blunt bangs and a sharp wit, and she's utterly out of her damn mind. She is three years older than me. A labor and delivery nurse by trade. Surfs waves. Mother of two.

So I have a sister who's a nurse and her husband, Heinz, is German, which provides endless amusement. 'Haven't the Jewish people suffered enough,' every time he skips doing the dishes, cries of 'Heil' when we say goodbye.

Shortly after meeting, Dana and I launched the 'HappyPussy Above All' project. A mission to please our hearts, pussies, and asses, where we harvest orgasms, rate, measure, and report back to each other. Horniness is our guiding light, and acting on it is the order of the day.

Dana and Heinz are polyamorous. She has a daughter with her husband and a second child we lovingly call 'lil' bastard,' born from a former lover. Heinz, our righteous gentile, adopted the boy as his own, and they're raising both children together as one holy and sort of happy family.

Heinz (when they're fighting, we call him 'Heinazi') runs yoga workshops across Europe, so his presence in Israel is off and on, emphasis on *off*. In recent years, he's juggled three relationships alongside Dana, also on and off, emphasis on *on*.

Lily, we love. She's Peruvian but lives in Austria. A descendant of a First Nations tribe with two thick black braids dangling from the sides of her beaming smile. Shakti-Parma, also a yoga teacher, lives in Pardes Hana. She used to be Emily before she saw the light, or maybe it was Heinz's magic wand. Donna Luisa is the third, a German from Dusseldorf, a Pilates instructor and facilitator of women's empowerment circles. We don't like her because she wants Heinz all to herself, to bear little neo-Nazi babies with him.

Since I met Dana, she's had a few lovers: a self-absorbed Tel Aviv businessman, a young, blond computer programmer, and a dreadlocked carpenter from the Galilee. He's the only one she's kept, because what he does with his little dick is nothing short of divine. After years of misguided assessments, we've discovered that small is best, bestie. It's the angle that makes the difference, not the length. Dana and I are defining the discipline of biological geometry.

At our last song circle, Isabelle, who is transgender, was there too, with catalog-picked tits no child will ever deflate. She had long, Rapunzel-like golden hair, talked like a woman and walked like a woman, but farted just like a man.

Inside the tent, before the bonfire, Isabelle sang the bible verse, "Who is the man that desireth life, and loveth days, that he may see good therein?" in a high, trembling voice.

I wondered aloud: "What about the woman? What if the woman desires life? Aren't there lyrics for that?"

"You're such a child," Dana whispered. "A woman doesn't desire, a woman Does."

"Does what she desires?" I asked.

"Desires life? Does life!" she answered.

"And if she's objectifidesired?" I pressed.

"Then she still does. Doesn't desire—doesn't do."

I still have much to learn. Maybe when I'm Dana's age I'll desire less and do more.

On Dana's last birthday, Lily, Heinz's lover, gifted her a jar of magic shrooms she had handpicked herself in an Austrian forest. The Rastafarian, Dana, and I gathered in his forest to munch them together. After marveling at the elephant that suddenly materialized on the path and climbing the rainbow that appeared between the trees, we returned to his caravan. He thought we'd have a threesome, but this isn't a brothel and I'm a conservative woman. All my children are from the same man, and I only sleep with other women. He can forget about it.

When my husband and I hit rough patches, Dana reminds me he's scatterbrained and sloppy. When Heinz overlooks her, despite her being right there, I'm there to remind her how very much she exists.

People sometimes mistake us for a couple because we're so close. My preferences are well-known, after all, but I'm not into incest. Lovers are plentiful, but a non-biological sister? She's the one and only.

# This Dick and The Man

He looks at me slyly. Naughty, perverted, and goal-oriented. The kids jump on him and he's plotting. We all eat together and he's plotting. He eyes me like a hungry tiger. Licks his lips. The kids jump. Get dirty. Ask for more water. He peels my clothes off with his eyes. We tend to them and play hunter and deer together. Someone will be prey. Someone will be eaten.

After we eat, we turn on the TV for them in the living room and announce that Mom and Dad are going to rest. I lock our bedroom door. I've barely turned the key when he charges at my body. Hungry and thirsty, he comes to me. I have honey to quench his thirst, a home for his longing.

We throw off underpants and shirts. He penetrates me. Arrives with a huge erection. Every time, I'm thrilled anew by the magic. All the blood flowing from his brain to his dick, elevating this marvelous creation. Holding it high, strong, proud. He enters me. Exits me. Enters and exits. His dick plays with my lower lips. Teases me. Gives everything and then pauses. I'm instantly wet. Wrap him in my—our—juices. So many years, I've been getting wet over him. So many years I open to him, his dick like an arrow at the bullseye of my life.

He pulls me to the bed and half-turns me. I lay on my side and he fucks me, stroking my legs. He says he admires my legs; I feel like he's fucking them. My stomach is soft and quivery, three kids ripped my skin apart and left me with stretch marks. His seed became flesh and blood within me and then tore my stomach apart. My tits are tired after six years of breastfeeding;

they move with the rhythm of the pumping. I manage to love myself this way. Through his dick, I love the blemishes that years have etched on me. Through his dick, I forgive my body for being tired, for aging, for looking more and more like my mother. He showers me with love, this dick and the man. He heals my soul's wounds when he accepts me like this, contains me like this. Fucks me sideways like this.

I don't know who invented the idea that women put out. It's the man who puts out and the woman, she can agree to accept.

I get into doggy position, on all fours, waiting for penetration, but he has other plans. He lies underneath me, his big face between my legs. Whiskers between my thighs. A strong, confident tongue pleasuring my clitoris. I ride his face like someone who knows the way.

"Touch yourself," I request. His right hand goes to his beautiful cock, his other hand on my ass, his face deep inside me, producing sounds of pleasure. I'm so turned on, watching his hand move on his dick, watching his forehead between my thighs, choking down the scream climbing up my body, shaking me from my vagina to my neck, from my clit to the deepest core of my bones. My body sways on his tongue. Inside my mind, flames rage between the wounds and the grandeur, the terror and despair of this life. I come. I give in to life. I choose it again. (And then he comes too. And then a nap. And then I wake him up and grab his dick, make him hard with my hand, climb him like an addict, like a fan, and I come again, strong and deep. He caresses my spine, going vertebra by vertebra and applying pressure between them. I'll always forgive him, I think to myself. I'll always consent to him because only with him am I me.)

# The Coordination of Passion

If you were here now, I'd take your hand and lead you to my bedroom. I'd close the door and press you against the wall. Not against your will, never coerced. But determined. I know what I want. Know what you want. Stomach to stomach. Forehead to forehead.

I'd shrink the distance between us, expand our closeness. Your lips. My lips. Thick, hot, sweet air between them. I'd press against your neck. Breathe in your skin, filling my lungs, softening years of longing within me.

I'd caress one shoulder, then the other, while my mouth kisses. The coordination of passion.

I'd kiss your neck. Your chin. Your beautiful collarbones. You'd open your mouth to me. Your voice would tell me this feels good to you. That you missed me too. You'd shudder against me. Purr with me. Whisper in my ear, "I love you. I missed you."

We've both used the same words for years, yet they can't contain all of this. They vanish at the sound of one sigh. A finger crosses exposed skin and all words melt away.

We'd go over to the bed. To lay on top of and underneath and beside each other. I'd lay straight, in circles, jagged with you. I'd fold myself into all the angles with you.

I'd peel more and more layers off you. Sweater of shame. Shirt of fear. Tank top of guilt. With every layer I take off, I'd tell you how beautiful you are like this. Determined, passionate. How much you're allowed to be.

I'd run my hand up and down the sides of your body. Caress your hourglass. Place a hand beneath the back of your neck. Skim my fingers along it. Kiss you on the lips. Soft. Touching not touching. Yes touching. Yes touching. You'd be discovered. Wrapping your legs around me, your hips swaying, thumping against me, singing songs to me. My heart knows how to keep a secret. My fingers know how to do holy work.

A green tsunami would wash over us both. Two cats in a big bed. "I love you," I'd whisper in your ear. On your cheek. In your mouth. "I love you," you'd say to my lips. To my chin. To my jaw. I'd eat you, licking, swallowing. I'd taste the grace of your soft skin, you'd cause an earthquake in me. I'd go up in flames with you, coming to you. I'd be left scorched earth after you.

# Vikram

When Amikam called to offer projects, I rarely refused. Each project required two or three weeks of preparation and a few days to execute. Maintaining the relationship afterward was simple, assisted by a basic Excel sheet: name, project, interaction dates, results.

The pay was high, commensurate with the risk. It allowed ample free time between projects. Three kids, a husband and an energetic dog were the obvious; Noga was the secret ingredient, but my deepest love, my real thrill, was longboard surfing. I started relatively late, at 37. Dana had urged me to try; I was convinced, took a lesson, and fell in love immediately. I was in the water every spare moment. I'd go to Bat Galim, Beit Yanai, wherever the swell took me.

The love of waves was addictive, leaving me strong and tanned even in winter. A long scar along my eye reminded me of a head-on collision with the surfboard when an east wind came in quickly. My eye socket was smashed, requiring two reconstructive surgeries. I never considered stopping.

The last project I accepted was interesting and ended successfully. Amikam asked me to meet with a division manager of an international energy company, an Indian man living in Kuwait with his wife and young daughter. As usual, I had to infect his computer with a program that would copy all his information, including typed passwords, to my computer. Amikam only provided details of the 'targets,' as he called them, reimbursed expenses, and paid the agreed amount. Beyond that, I was solely responsible for achieving the desired outcome.

Amikam was interested in plans to apply for tenders and financial models, which I provided in exchange for the small fortune he paid me. But I was most interested in their small, dirty secrets—and there were always, always a few.

The Indian target's name was Vikram. I made contact under the guise of a human resources professional with a management role to offer him in Switzerland. I already had an active profile on LinkedIn and a headhunting website I'd maintained for years. This was my favorite game. People struggled to turn down the idea of relocating to Europe and funding their children's education at an American school. After a few phone calls, we set a date to meet the next time he was in London. It took about a month of schmoozing, but we finally met.

I rented an office by the hour in central London to interview him for the position. I prepared a presentation for a water desalination company seeking a European division CEO. Reverse osmosis. Employee roster. Expected growth. Potential partnerships with leading companies. Easy.

Vikram, with a bulbous nose and thinning hair, arrived dressed in a suede suit that was an artificial green color with golden dragon cufflinks. He turned out to be a brilliant and charming man. We greeted each other warmly, and he was eager to hear about the new opportunity. Immediately after the first slide, my computer suddenly shut off and I couldn't restart it. I tried repeatedly, embarrassed and apologizing for the technical difficulties.

After several failed attempts, I asked, "Perhaps we could view the presentation on your computer?"

He smiled, "Sure, sure," and I inserted the flash drive into the designated port, uploading the presentation onto his laptop.

I presented the company and the profile of the intended CEO, trying to be articulate, serious, and include a touch of humor. I'd practiced this presentation dozens of times at home, and Vikram's pleasant demeanor made the game enjoyable. He said it sounded interesting and that he'd be happy to move forward. We agreed to stay in touch and said goodbye with a handshake.

In my hotel room, I poured a glass of white wine from the minibar and turned on my laptop. I inserted the infected USB and entered the password. Lines and lines started scrolling across the computer: websites Vikram had visited, engineering plan files, drawings, contracts, his viewing history. That's where I found it. Muscular black men fucking each other, individually or in groups. Namaste, Vikram! I smiled to myself and closed my computer.

*Virginia My Love*

*Every woman needs a lover of her own*
*Or a female lover, in my case.*
*Every woman needs a perch to lay her head,*
*To nestle her breast,*
*To let her cunt rest.*

*Every woman needs a window with a moon*
*A succulent plant*
*Sweet fruit on the tongue*
*A joint rolled between the lips*
*And nails to dig into the back of her hand when the pain burns.*

*Every woman needs a space without children*
*Without neighbors*
*To scream*
*Until she's hoarse*
*To cry with no remorse.*

*Every woman needs to delay her orgasm*
*Until she no longer can*
*And then let it burst forth*
*Like she's deranged*
*Without being disturbed.*

# She Cooks Me Like Sweet Caramel

Seven in the evening and we approach each other hesitantly. Reaching out after seven days and nights apart. How do we rebuild this bridge, this relationship, anew each time?

We sit and talk on the couch. Close, so close. She strokes my shoulder and collarbone. "The most beautiful clavicle in the world," she says. She pulls my bra strap and tank top spaghetti strap aside so they don't interfere with her caressing my skin. I graze her leg. It doesn't tickle or annoy her, a good sign.

She lifts my tank top over my head and I reach behind my back in a practiced movement to unhook my bra. My breasts are freed. "Come here for a hug," she says, spreading her arms.

"This is the couch where we first hugged," I remind her. This is where I entered an embrace I haven't wanted to leave for two years now.

She removes her dress, staying in her underwear. Nice satin ones I bought her, underwear her husband saw and then asked if I'd bought the same for myself. The answer is no, but he's smart, her husband. I did buy us matching underwear, but a different set. These, I knew, would look especially nice on her ass.

She leans back against the couch's armrest, white upper body with pink nipples. I'm in well-worn capri jeans, my upper body exposed. I lay on her. My head is next to her stomach, raised so I can talk to her. Her head looks at me, orange and burning and smart. Her skin is soft and smells like her, like my once-a-week home. My heart's storage unit.

"I had a hard week," she said, "you were so with him."
I try to unpack this with her. "I'm here too," I tell her.

And she says, "Now go down on me," with determination. I move toward her groin and she discards her underwear. Says: "Take off your jeans, it's not appropriate to go down on me in jeans." I rise from the couch, quickly remove them, and return to her body, but not her vagina. Not immediately. I make her wait. She'll get what she wants, but not yet.

I lick her belly button in circles. Kiss the soft area between her navel and pubic hair. There's ample space for kissing there, and the night is young. Her breathing intensifies, her hips move; I can feel her getting wet against me, but it's not time yet.

I kiss her pubic bone. Don't enter yet. I move between her legs, gently spreading them. She resists and I push. She responds, opening wider. I lick the tendons in her thighs. Bite her strong, soft, round thighs. I lick, bite, hold tight, and she's already squirming. She wants me in her vagina, she burns for me, but I want to drive her crazy a bit longer.

I move to her other thigh. I lick. Suck. Bite. She moans. She doesn't flinch or say it tickles, so I understand that today I can dive deep. Her body is open, to me and to herself.

After teasing her thighs, I arrive at the holiest of holies, at god's sanctuary. I run a long tongue over her outer lips. Then over her inner lips. Lightly lick her clitoris then go back to her lips. I know she wants me on her clitoris. I know she's yearning. I deliberately pause my tongue. Lick it and then leave it. Lick it exactly on the hood, a bit back, a bit under, where it drives her particularly wild, and then pause again. Leave there again, lick along her vagina's opening. Kiss with little pecks.

I give-don't give, let her arousal build, until I decide it's time and my tongue attaches to her clitoris and doesn't let go. I lick it from different angles, gently and more firmly. Lick side to side and up and down.

She makes sounds of pleasure. I place two fingers at her vulva's opening but don't enter yet. She sways on my mouth, this wild sex goddess attached to my lips. I feel like praying to her.

My fingers rest at the lower opening of her vulva, pressing slightly, my tongue working her clitoris with full force. Her voice grows louder, she grunts at me and I feel streaks of wetness down my thighs. I slowly, ever so slowly, penetrate her warm, tight body with my fingers. I do it gently, checking with every millimeter that I'm welcome. I'm so welcome.

She's wet, she's sweating, she's swaying from side to side. I enter her in slow motion until my two fingers are inside her, then I move my hand while pleasuring her with my tongue and mouth.

I lap up her juices, the sounds from her sweet mouth making me melt. Yes, my love, yes. It's all yours, all the pleasure in the world—is yours. She arches her back, moves her head side to side, closes her eyes, grips my hand tightly while I fuck her with it and with my mouth. She moves faster and faster. Her vagina tightens around my hand in little contractions. I continue. She brushes my hair aside and looks at me. I lick her and look at her, lift my neck and offer my eyes. Between us a white belly, small tits, and a world of love. I lick and look and the entire universe is between us. I keep licking and fucking her with my hand. She moves toward me and says, "It's a problem because I'll never tell you to stop." I continue. I have no intention of stopping. She can make my dreams come true and let me go on for hours. Until the alarm goes off and our time is up. Even then, I'll still desire her.

We move in waves. I'm inside her and she surrenders, her head tilted back now, eyes closed. She yells again and again, each time louder. She takes my free hand and puts it on her right hand. I hold on tight. Not gentle this time, I cover her entire breast with my hand and keep licking and moving my fingers in her. She yells louder, grunts, grabs the couch pillow tightly. She hurts my hand when she squeezes it. She cries out her pleasure and excites me as she comes so hard.

"I'm turning around," she tells me, and I unlatch my tongue from her clitoris but leave my fingers inside her. She turns slowly, so we don't come undone. She lies on her stomach, her beautiful, white ass in front of my face, two of my fingers still inside her. I continue the fucking motion. My hand looks like a gun with two pointed fingers and I pump them back and forth in her. I shoot all our fears. I shoot everyone who is against us. I fiercely protect our love.

My face is across from this round, white ass and I kiss and lick it. I'm careful, attentive to see if she jumps because it tickles, but she doesn't. I nip at her ass, biting it again and again, reminding myself not to leave marks.

She moves her pelvis against me and I move my hand inside her, my teeth in her flesh, and she reaches out to take my hand and places it in front, on her clitoris. I feel her between my two hands. Feel her hip bones, the warmth of her vagina, her passion between my two hands. She comes in a wave and then whispers, "More."

"Yes," I answer her, "more." She continues to press her clitoris with my hand, my other hand fucking her hard.

She comes again and when the orgasm is over she cries, unburdening her heart here next to me. Her body shakes. I'm still inside her. She turns around to me. I come up to her face level and look in her eyes, my fingers still inside her. Only when I have settled in comfortably next to her do I pull them out slowly, gently. Her crying intensifies. She sobs and I hold her arm. I don't comfort or encourage. I don't want to interfere. She licks my face like a wounded animal. Looks in my eyes again and again.

"I cry just from you looking at me," she says. "Don't leave me."

"I'm not leaving," I say to her.

"You thought about it. You left me once." She cries and cries, and laughs at how much she's crying.

"Hey, you're getting me wet," I say to her and she bursts out in huge laughter. She cries our pain. She cries our distance. I always leave her a little. "We already broke up once," she says, "in a different incarnation. You died on me. Maybe you were a soldier. You left me." She bursts out crying again. "You see why I don't need drugs?" she asks. "Life is the strongest substance for me."

I say to her: "If I met you on MDMA, I would think—who is this broken person," and again she bursts out laughing. I love her laughing. She laughs fully from her heart and her throat, like a little girl, like a crazy woman. I love her crying. She feels everything, she's not afraid of hurting. I'm jealous of her for that.

"When you were going down on me, I saw animals," she tells me. "I saw predators, I saw birds of prey and a gazelle. I saw an enormous whale. I myself was a whale and I swam deep in the water." I listen and look at her, and my eyes must make her sad again because she cries again. She asks if it's okay with me, she has more to get out. I get up naked and get her tissue. She blows her nose and apologizes for the noise.

"Don't apologize," I say to her. She's so sweet, good God.

She calms down and we talk a bit about the week that went by. How far we were. How good it is to be together. She caresses my closed thighs, tries to find a way, a path, between them. I stay closed, letting her try a bit longer and, a second before she gets frustrated, I spread my legs open. She slips easily into my wet vagina. She moans, "Being inside of you is a dream I didn't dare dream," she says. She starts making fucking motions and gets closer to kiss my clitoris. Her tongue is good to me, her hands know me. My legs spread wide in her honor, inviting her to a celebratory party. She licks me, penetrates me, moves in me and I feel streams of fire from the soles of my feet to the tip of my head. She stops using her tongue and continues using only her hand. God, how is it that she knows how to fuck me. Her hand is strong, determined.

I remember how surprised I was the first few times by this combination, such a gentle woman with such wild power.

She really is a bird of prey, I think to myself, moving inside of me like a determined falcon. She fucks me hard, on the edge of pain.

She doesn't let up, doesn't worry, she's fast and tough, deconstructing places in me that have hardened over the years.

She lifts my hips up and I'm almost in the air, only the soles of my feet and my shoulder blades touch the couch. She caresses my ass from below and fucks me hard with her fingers and I lose myself in space. Her hand directs me, fills me, exists as a point of reference in free space. I go back to laying on the couch with my legs lifted, apart. I beg for her to come to me, to sit with her vagina on my face, but she doesn't. She looks at me and keeps fucking. Painful. Hard. Healing. She exorcises my demons this way, she puts red love in black places. She cooks me like sweet caramel, I have to be careful not to burn between her hands.

The alarm goes off. In fifteen minutes I'll have to leave. Shit. Shit. I reach over to turn it off. I beg again, "Come to me," and she agrees. Maybe because of the clock. I pull her to me so that I'm lying on my side and she's lying on her side, her mouth and hand inside me, my mouth and hand inside her. With my other hand I hold her body close, close to mine, holding her face, her hair. She licks my fingers and goes back to licking my vagina.

I go crazy from her vagina in my face. From the smell, the texture, the moisture, from this sensation that isn't like anything else.

I go crazy from her tongue in my pussy, and I can't hold it back anymore.

I feel the orgasm coming, strong and overwhelming, it washes over all of me. Afterwards come soft orgasmic ripples that slowly calm me down. I keep hugging her tight, my face between her legs, her face on my thighs. We are one. We will soon have to separate, but for now we are together.

We rise, still shellshocked. We need to get dressed. She goes into the bathroom, and I fix the pillows on the couch.

I follow her into the bathroom where she's getting dressed, putting her pretty dress back on and filling a water bottle for her drive home. She fixes her hair. "Do I look okay?" she asks. Her husband will be awake when she returns, he can't fall asleep without her. She's worried that he'll see on her how good she has it with me. She's worked up, and we're out of time.

"You're beautiful, my love," I tell her.

I put my jeans and black tank top back on. We leave the studio tidy. I hope the pillows on the couch will be dry by tomorrow and the sharp smell of pussy will dissipate. We say goodbye hastily but stop for a wet, long kiss, biting a bit, pulling at each other's lips a bit. I get into my car, she gets into hers. I roll down the window and mouth to her so as not to yell: I love you. She answers me with no sound, I love you.

I drive home. Take the joint I prepared ahead of time out of the glovebox. Light it and drive slowly, following the law. I drive 87 kilometers per hour all the way home, a good girl for the Israeli police. Music plays from my Spotify. My vagina is swollen, hurts a little.

It will take another week before we meet again, the countdown begins. I take a deep breath and turn the imaginary hourglass on its head.

# Cloud Kisses

I am lying down and you are lying on top of me, your entire body pressed against mine. I feel our chests, stomachs, and thighs kissing each other. We are entwined, as close as humanly possible.

We exchange soft, cloud kisses as I inhale your scent deeply. You descend with your body and kisses, licking the length of me. From my face to my neck. From my neck to my collarbone. Long strokes with your juicy, mischievous tongue.

Your tongue speaks to my skin, reciting love poems. You linger on my tits, your tongue conversing with them at length. You are lick-licking and I'm already as wet as a Norwegian fjord. You trace my stomach, holding me in your hands, your licks ever-changing. Soft, fluttery, strong. You vary the rhythm, keeping me alert.

You play with your tongue and I am, accordingly, a plaything in your mouth, between your hands. You kiss, lick me, your mouth on my yearning-for-you skin. The wetness of your mouth on my body dripping with longing. You lick your way down my thighs. My legs have long been spread wide. My vagina screams her desire for you, but you leave her burning like a raging bonfire while you lick my thighs, the area all around my vagina, then ascend the slope of my thighs again.

My vagina senses your face nearby, your heart close to my pulse, your body tight against me, tempting and soft. She begs for you, but you return to my face for more soft kisses of grace. You're lick-licking my mouth, my tongue dancing with yours.

You rise and offer your breast to my mouth. I'm overwhelmed by your generosity. My mouth feels you and the air between my legs ignites. You're so close, so beautiful above me.

You resume licking my thighs and turn me over to lick their other side. I lie on my stomach. Each lick sends shivers through me. My nipples are erect, my skin covered in goosebumps, swans, sensitive and airy toward you.

Your tongue glides up my ass cheeks. My vagina roars for you and you hear her, but you don't give it to me yet. You trace up my back with your licks, occasionally biting, and I arch, rave, meet you as tigress to tigress, back to stomach, heart to heart.

You make your way back to my mouth with licks and kisses, forging a route that is ours alone. I feel your tits on my back, your hair, your tongue. You draw a topographical map of love on me, paving a wordless path with your mouth.

You lie down on my back and kiss me, deep and wet. I'm immobile, I lie there, surrendering. Do whatever you want, do, touch, do me.

You take my finger and guide it into your vagina, the temple of my heart. I moan, awash with gratitude. I wet your bed and plead with you. And then, only then, do you penetrate me.

# Hong Kong

When Amikam called to offer me the new project, I hesitated. The target was the strategic planning manager of a massive Chinese electronic components manufacturer, and I felt uneasy about it from the start.

"Please consider it," Amikam pleaded.

One more successful job and I could fulfill my dream: surfing Hawaii's beaches, gliding between Waikiki and Poipu on endless waves under the warm sun. The money tempted me, Hawaii beckoned from the future, but I dreaded working with Chinese targets. They were hard to read, and my stomach churned at the thought of what might happen if I were to be exposed.

After a sleepless night weighing the pros and cons, I told Amikam, "I'll do it. But this is my last project. After this, I'm out."

"We'll see," Amikam replied, launching straight into the briefing. "The company's CEO is Brian Wang." Brian, my ass— as much as I'm Princess Diana, I thought. "Our client is a semiconductor manufacturer. They'll pay for everything you get: drawings, formulas, costs." Yeah, I know the drill.

I approached Wang posing as an HR manager seeking a CEO for a major Singaporean company, but he rebuffed all my attempts to meet. He insisted he was happy in Taiwan and uninterested in exploring other opportunities. Through his secretary, he made it clear he was too busy for my calls, and to please stop calling if possible.

I started preparing the alternative plan, after which my connection with him could be burned, but hopefully I wouldn't be.

I decided to meet Wang at a conference in Hong Kong, an annual international conference for technology and electronic components trade. I registered for the conference as the owner of an HR firm. Participation in the conference cost 3,200 dollars, the flights and hotel another 2,500 dollars. This was going to be an expensive experiment, and I only had one chance.

I hope you're worth it, Brian superstar. I felt a rush of adrenaline and I reminded myself, as I did every time I got nervous, that I myself had pushed an entire person out of my body, more than once. "Yougotthisyougotthisyougotthis," I muttered the magic spell that I've adopted for myself.

I flew to Hong Kong and bought a cellphone and local SIM card with cash. I had business cards printed with a fake email address and the new number.

On the conference's first day, I arrived early to the networking breakfast. Orange juice sparkled in tall wine glasses as I scanned the room for Wang. These Chinese businessmen all fucking blurred together, but Wang, according to online photos, had a mole on his left cheek and a smug look in his eyes, like a little pervert.

After an hour of circling, I spotted him. I hung back, observing from a distance. As a tall Western woman amidst a sea of men in suits, I stood out. Used to the attention, I maintained my distance, flashing my most dazzling smile—the one that concealed a world of curses beneath it.

In the evening, I wore a red dress with a plunging neckline and the big gold necklace I had inherited from my grandmother—my lucky charm. I piled my hair high, letting a few rebellious strands escape. I doused myself in perfume; there's no such thing as too much. I applied smoky eye shadow close to my temple and along my eyelid crease, accentuating my already large, round eyes.

I called reception and booked a massage for nine-thirty the

following night. Then I headed back down to the lobby for cocktail hour. I quickly spotted Wang again, bantering with other Chinese businessmen in suits. It looks like a video game, I thought to myself. I felt like mowing them all down with a machine gun, one by one.

I ran my hand along my hip, smoothing my dress. Taking a deep breath, I approached him, wine glass in hand and a megawatt smile plastered on my face.

Wang smiled at me, his gaze deep down my neckline. As my research had suggested, he was no gentleman.

"Nice to meet you. Monique," I said, with a slight French accent, offering my hand.

"Brian," he replied with a Chinese accent, "Brian Wang."

He shook my hand, his palm limp and clammy against mine. I giggled.

"What brings you to the conference?"

He launched into telling me about his position, innovation, inspiration. He prattled on about demanding Western clientele, overweight Americans who act like they own Asia. "They look like hungry piggies," he whispered in my ear, and I threw my head back with ringing laughter.

He said I had beautiful eyes.

"Me?? Really?? Thanks." I smiled shyly, averting my gaze as if it were the first time a man had ever paid me a compliment.

His predictability was embarrassing.

"So, what are you doing here?" he asked.

"I'm friends with Pierre, the hotel manager," I replied. "I'm his guest. I only attend the big, important conferences. Entomology gatherings don't interest me."

He laughed heartily, too much so. I noticed his yellowing teeth, counting five silver fillings. His face was naturally smooth, the mole on his left cheek bumpy up close.

I leaned in, as if sharing a secret: "I run a call girl company."

His filthy eyes widened—I'd found my way in. "You know what, let me tell you all about it tomorrow evening. Nine o'clock in your room? Are you staying here?"

"Yes. Room 1308."

"I'll be there."

We clinked glasses. "Ganbei," we said, sipping while maintaining eye contact. I turned and headed for my room, walking straight ahead without a sideways glance. With each step, I felt his eyes on my back.

In my room, I video-called Tom and the kids, who seemed so far from me, worlds away. Michaela had just written a rhyming poem about dragons, and Lev waved at the screen, sticky orange popsicle dripping down his little fingers. Suddenly, I missed them fiercely. Breathe, I reminded myself, you're only halfway there.

The next morning, I took time for myself. I walked to Victoria Harbor, then took the ferry to Kowloon Peninsula to capture the city's absurd, exhilarating skyline. I bought gifts for each of the kids, and the smartwatch Tom had requested—the one that monitors your heart rate. I treated myself to a new dress before returning to the hotel in the afternoon. I tried to take a short nap, but sleep eluded me. I was too excited, there was too much at stake.

At six, I rose. My heart raced. To calm my nerves, I poured a glass of white wine from the minibar, limiting myself to just one before nine o'clock. I inhaled deeply, nose in the glass. I waited for the wine's flavor to oxygenate and unfold. I had time.

I remembered to text Tom, asking if he'd given the dog its medicine. The wound on its front leg had almost healed when I left; I didn't want any setbacks. He confirmed that he had, in fact, remembered.

I stepped into the shower, washing my hair and soaping my body before aiming the strong stream between my legs. I began fantasizing about Tom's cock, how he'd take me from behind. My imagination shifted—I had a dick, and Wang's ass was exposed to me. "I'll fuck you up the ass," I whispered in my mind, beginning to penetrate him with my imaginary erection. Abruptly, I shook off the thought. Fuck you being fucked by me! I'm not letting you into my fantasies—you wish.

I let the orgasm slip away, abandoning it, then refocused. This technique always helps when I'm struggling to come. I conjured the flight attendant's face from my recent flight—her lips painted a soft pink, her slightly slanted eyes blending with Tom's cock, Noga's freckled arms, and the imaginary dick between my legs. I felt both penetrator and penetrated, my breath quickening until I experienced a powerful, calming orgasm. I immediately shut off the water and stepped out.

I dressed unhurriedly, slipping on the black dress I'd bought earlier. In Hong Kong, I'm a size large. They're petite, these Asian women, to match their men's small dicks. Nature is always clever. I admired my new dress, knowing it would serve me well in the future too.

I packed, dropped my suitcase at reception and, at five past nine, I knocked on room 1308. Those five minutes were crucial; he needed to wait a bit. He answered wearing only his work pants. His chest was smooth like a young boy's, with a small, sagging belly. His arrogant smile unfurled like a self-narrating story. You're revolting, I thought, flashing him a wide, toothy smile.

"May I come in?" I asked in my slight French accent. He smiled, deliberately leaving not enough space between himself and the doorframe.

I brushed past him, my breasts grazing his smooth chest through my dress. For a fleeting moment, I could hear the waters of Waikiki as a wave rose behind me, but I snapped back to the present. It was showtime; I couldn't afford to waste a second.

I sat in the armchair and placed my laptop on the TV stand beside me.

"Would you like a drink?" he asked.

"Sure," I answered. "Jack, please."

He poured me a generous Jack Daniels in a lowball glass. He handed it to me and sat across from me on the bed, drink in hand. He was barefoot and, oddly, his feet looked beautiful to me. Delicate yet strong.

I told him about the services offered by Dolphin, the company I'd founded, in my sweet French accent. We have 102 girls, not just in Asia, I hinted at international success and global fucking. "Our girls are top-tier, available in pairs or trios. Western students trying to cover the high tuition costs in Hong Kong. Americans, Australians. We have a beautiful Romanian economics student, and a nursing student from Moldova."

He didn't question why she'd study nursing in Hong Kong, which was admittedly a stupid idea, but the concept of the merciful nurse is so potent that I didn't hesitate to use it.

"Let me show you my presentation," I said, opening my laptop. After the first slide, the computer suddenly froze. I feigned surprise, apologizing profusely. "This has never happened before," I said. "*Merde*. What should we do? Do you have a laptop here, perhaps? I have such an amazing catalogue, I can have someone gorgeous here for you in an hour." Then I smiled as if struck by inspiration: "The first time is on me, because you've been such a sweetheart, *mon cheri*," I said, eyeing his body suggestively. "You'll have such a good time, I'm sure you'll want us for all your upcoming conferences. Think of it as an investment in our future relationship."

His silver fillings glinted as he smiled. He rose and retrieved his laptop from the closet, and I inserted my flash drive. My heart rate spiked, but I maintained my composure. I took a small sip of whiskey. The end was in sight.

I walked him through the presentation I'd meticulously crafted over the past week. It featured photos I'd sourced from the internet, each girl assigned a serial number and a brief, fabricated backstory. I emphasized the two blondes who came as a pair; I could tell by Wang's eyes and his eager smile that they excited him. I finished the presentation. I could detect his arousal through the mingled scents of alcohol and aftershave. Surging testosterone has its own distinct odor.

The phone I'd bought two days ago rang. It took me a moment to recognize the unfamiliar ringtone. I answered—it was reception informing me that they were waiting for me at the spa. It was nine-thirty. I replied, "I'll be right there, I'm leaving now."

"I have to take care of an urgent matter," I told Wang abruptly, standing up. I quickly unplugged my flash drive from his computer and left him holding my business card.

"Call me. Actually, give me your number," I said, punching in the digits as he recited them, slightly dazed by the sudden turn of events. "I'll handle this and then see about getting you someone amazing for tonight. *Au revoir*, Brian." Before he could respond, I blew him an air kiss, slipped out of room 1308, and pressed the elevator button.

As the elevator doors closed behind me, my heart suddenly started racing. I collected my suitcase from reception, paid for the massage I never received, and asked the desk clerk to call me a taxi to the airport.

"Certainly, madame," he replied.

In the taxi's backseat, my heart still pounding, I opened my laptop. I connected to the internet via my phone's hotspot and entered my password. Lines of text began scrolling down the screen. Patent registrations. Code snippets. His internet browsing history. Gangbang porn. Boom! I thought to myself. Fucking boom.

I changed in a large airport bathroom stall. Jeans. Flat shoes. I left my makeup on. I sent Brian Wang a message apologizing: I had to go to the police station because of a sweet employee who has gotten into trouble. Don't ask, *mon cheri*, it's best that you not contact me in the near future. As he was typing a reply, I removed the phone's battery and tossed it in one trash bin, then walked a few steps and threw the phone itself into another.

I settled into the airport lounge, reopened my computer, and started sifting through Wang's files, downloading commercial plans. Who's fucking who now, Mister Wang? Did you say something? Oh sorry, I couldn't hear you, the breeze in Waikiki is just skimming my face as drops of water break in the sunlight.

I messaged Amikam that the fox had been trapped, and texted Tom that I was on my way home, asking him to turn on the water heater for me in the morning. Only then did I allow myself to relax, ordering a large Jack Daniels in a lowball glass.

*My Fucker*

*He is never mine*
*Turning outward, upward*
*He is a hawk and an ox in his threshing*
*Plowing my earth, the sharp-eyed bird of prey*
*That hunted me until I wallowed in blood.*

*I want to swallow his seed, his power*
*Yearning for his spirit.*
*Thirsty for his gaze*
*I want the sparks of his mane upon me*
*Always desperate for him, forever.*

*Contorting shapes to create friction*
*In fire and pillars of smoke I understand*
*Dragging him to a battle of dark spirits*
*The boxing ring of the soul.*

*From his cock came life*
*From his mouth spilled words*
*That wove me crowns, that drilled holes in me.*
*He is, he is not,*
*Never mine.*

## Like Lightning

Tonight we have the house to ourselves. Quiet, clean. She undresses me on the couch. I lie on top of her, naked. She's wearing a dress. She caresses me. Gazes at me. My legs are slightly parted, my tanned knee on her pale leg. I love myself, how I look through her eyes.

Our kisses fizz like Pop Rocks in our mouths. Her lips are pink marshmallows. Her dress comes off swiftly, followed by her bra and underwear. She asks me to lie on my stomach. I'm naked, obedient, and so wet. She's beside me on the couch, her hand finds its way to my pussy, enters me. I swallow her in, I have to feel her inside. I'm hungry, needy, and unapologetic.

She penetrates me gently, grunting together with me. She feels everything that I experience. I'm so contained, I'm so free. She licks me from behind. Penetrates me with her tongue and I moan. I open before her like a clam. Between the two halves of the shell, I am quivering tissue. I'm wet, a silky thickness flowing over her fingers.

I want to be delicious for her, beautiful for her. I celebrate myself into her eyes, so that she may delight in me. I hear her taking pleasure, she makes sounds for me so that I can see the way. She doesn't know it, but this is how she releases verdant fields within me. Her pleasure from me opens a gate to vast spaces inside me, and there are galloping mares, deer. I gallop on the palm of her hand, I am a mare in the fields.

I am turned on by her closeness, by her intertwining with me, by the one wetness we are. She waves me like the sea, and I swirl in a thick, invisible current. God, her tongue. What she does to me. How does she know? How is it possible for her to mix me up this way? I don't know any more if my head is up or down. There is no up or down here, this is an intergalactic 360-degree space, and it's in me or in her or in the slippery connection of her tongue and my clitoris.

She pushes herself so that her head is underneath my pussy. Now she's lying on the couch and I sit with my pussy on her mouth. I lean against the armrest of the couch, petting her head. She's beautiful, the entire length of her, with her playful eyes, with her white lioness nose inside the black of my pussy. Her maple-sweet tongue coils around my clitoris and her hand is inside me. I move on her, she is in me and on me.

My orgasm is enormous. Shakes the walls of my vulva and the foundations of my soul. I yell loudly, expressing through my voice the tornado that floods me. At the end of the waves of the orgasm, I burst out crying. Air leaves my lungs quickly, I gasp. I can feel how they are leaving me with every exhale: the pain, the yearning, the endless missing. They leave until there's nothing left. I am not anymore. I have no scars. I'm a newborn baby learning to breathe. I relax into her, more.

She bites my shoulder hard, and a chill runs through me like lightning in my pussy. I close my teeth on her collarbone. I stay on top her, my open mouth against her body, like a dog in heat. I breathe her in deeply, into my pores. We rearrange ourselves, holding each other close on the couch. She looks into my eyes. I look back, my eyes wide with happiness and terror. It's flagrantly irresponsible to forfeit my heart this way.

I want to speak, but I'm unable. Words are swallowed in my throat. Her hand caresses my hair. I bury my head in her stomach and keep descending. Everything I cannot express is served to her pussy through my silent tongue.

## My Extractions

I lie on the examination table, the lower half of my body exposed. The cold metallic speculum spreads my cervix open. Tom stands behind me, clutching my right hand tightly. It hurts. Three times he has hurt me this way—at our children's births.

The doctor sits before me, between my legs, perched on a high, black, wheeled chair with a round seat and no backrest.

To my left is a white-painted brick wall. The gaps between the bricks are wide and gray. My left hand grasps at them, feeling their industrial, rough texture. The doctor inserts a large, thick plastic syringe into me. He explains each step, detailing what is happening and what will happen next. I sense his respect for me and my body. Respect and warmth we've purchased for 4,500 shekels. In an envelope. Cash. He asks if the pain is bearable.

"Yes," I reply, feeling a tug in my stomach.

"It will get more painful," he warns.

The doctor extracts the contents of my womb. Tom squeezes one hand while the other clenches around a white brick on the wall. The pulling is relentless, the pain excruciating. I wanted this abortion, I chose it, but my womb screams, burning with agony.

I want to kick the doctor, yell at him and Tom: Don't touch my children! Don't you dare take them! But I remain silent. Instead, tears stream down my face. I grip the brick tighter, desperate to feel anything but my abdomen. I know that relaxing would ease the pain. If I let the children go, it would hurt less, but I can't.

I resist strenuously, contracting around the syringe as if trying to fight it, knowing I have no chance of winning.

The doctor finishes. The syringe emerges, filled with a yellowish, cloudy liquid flecked with blood clots. These are my fetal children, the twins who came to me. Whether they have souls, I don't know, but I'm certain my soul is forever stained with their blood. When the doctor announces we're done and Tom releases my hand, I slide off the examination table, feeling immediate relief. It's over. The dilemma has passed; I'm no longer torn between my head and my heart.

I dress slowly, my movements gentle and shaky, as if recovering from an accident. I ask the doctor if the nausea will subside now. I've thrown up so much in the past few days. He assures me, "Yes, your body will gradually realize it's no longer pregnant." We schedule a follow-up for the next week.

Three days post-abortion. Lev woke multiple times during the night. I managed only three hours of sleep. Tom slept for nine; I know because I lay awake beside him. The alarm sounds, and I ask Tom to tend to the kids and let me sleep. It's perhaps the third time in my life I've made such a request. It is a testament to my fragile state. I am exhausted and sad. Tom, still groggy, fails to understand. He asks me to wake him up again in five minutes, as if I'm the snooze button. I make an unhappy face and rise from bed defiantly, thinking: With this kind of support, who needs favors?

He gets up immediately after me, saying: "No need for that face. I said I'd get up for them, I just asked for five minutes."

This is his consistent complaint: my demeanor in the mornings, my facial expressions. "A calm morning," he insists, "is crucial for starting my workday." I wonder if I'm the problem here, if a calm morning with three children is even possible.

We get over this bump, organize the kids, and drop them off at preschool, at school. Upon returning, we resume our argument.

"How could you not let me sleep?" I ask. "You slept three times as long as I did."

"I would have gotten up," he counters. "I only asked for five minutes. You have such a negative vibe at home; I don't think you realize how much. Maybe you need psychiatric medication. You don't understand how your attitude makes the entire household suffer."

I freeze. Stop all movement. Stop the conversation. Tears constrict my throat, nearly choking me. I'm bleeding. I slept for three non-consecutive hours. I'm heartbroken by the massacre that occurred, that is still occurring, within my body. Did he really just say that to me?

For three years, I've been the primary caregiver. Tom earns good money and lives like a sheik at home. We created a distorted gender dynamic where his work is sacrosanct, and I'm the woman behind the successful man. With our third child's birth, I—who completed my degrees before him, who once out-earned him—became, by choice, a homemaker.

I'm the big mama to our children, the one who nursed for long distances, the one who is there for every significant moment—basketball practices, skinned knees, lost teeth. I'm the woman available to be fucked 24/7, who translates whatever he needs into English, who adorns his arm in a red dress at consular events, who does the laundry and cooks his meals, offering compassion and care to all, who gets up at night, who enabled his ascent to important manager and successful senior executive.

I halt everything. Something fundamental shifted in me forever on that examination table. "I can't do this anymore," I tell him. "This dynamic ends now." I refuse to be addressed this way, to be drained of all I have to give. Quietly, I pack a bag: clothes, toiletries, my computer and charger, a book. He speaks as I pack, asking me to listen, begging for forgiveness. I don't really know what he is saying, because I'm not really listening. I'm listening to me now.

I'm at my mom's. Bleeding. Everything aches, but I feel more clarity than ever. Tom sends lengthy, loving text messages. Like an abusive husband, he too is gifted at reconciliation. He writes that he understands, vows never to argue about mornings again. Writes that I deserve to sleep. That I'm allowed to make faces. He promises to change.

My mother, ever graceful, navigates unpleasantness with poise, emerging unscathed and smiling. This woman, who never dirties her hands, opens her home to me. She's very eager for reconciliation. Tom calls her too, tells her that he'll take care of himself and says that it's hard to admit, but he does need therapy. This impresses her; she too succumbs to his charm again and again. Like a battered woman, I forgive him and return home, but something within me is different. I know it. He doesn't yet.

Three more days pass. Six days post-abortion, I'm still bleeding rivers of blood. A minor argument erupts one morning. Tom ignites, within seconds shouting at me in front of the children: "Leave, you whore! Go to Noga."

I freeze, staring at him. The three children I have in this world are here—witnessing this filth spewing from his mouth. I remain silent in the face of his rage. For the first time, I don't retaliate with my own violent anger. For the first time, I disengage from this crazy and dangerous game.

For years, we've been trapped in this cycle. Hellish fights, heavenly passion. I always told my girlfriends: "Our bad is gloriously bad, but the good... is so damn good." For years, I believed that because we were both fire, we fought and fucked with equal passion, and nothing could change that.

Luna and Lev, our youngest, cover their ears with their tiny hands. They've learned to do this themselves now. When they were younger, Michaela, the oldest, would cover Lev's ears, and she taught Luna to protect, at least this sense. If I responded to Tom, Michaela would plead with me to stop. She'd beg me: "Don't answer him, don't answer him, don't answer him." I heard her, but didn't listen. We were busy with our rage; she interfered with our igniting the fire in each other's souls. She tries again now: "Mom, don't answer him."

I'm different now. I'm resolute that these children won't witness this anymore. They won't experience this violence and verbal abuse, these outbursts of hatred and my humiliation. They won't see me losing control at the insults I absorb, won't see me breaking because of him and cursing him in return. It's over.

Quietly, I usher the kids into the car. They're stunned, silent, solidifying together into a single mass of obedience. He pounds on the car door. "Now you're going to turn this into a big deal?" he yells. "Now, because of that one word that slipped out, you won't let me forget it, will you?" I don't respond. I'm broken and bleeding, weak and thin, but stronger than ever. I'm not afraid. I extracted my own children from my body. I wielded a knife and drew the boundary between us with blood—between me and them. Between life and death. Between the children who are here and those who are gone. Nothing in this world can frighten me now.

I drive away, soothing the children as I take them to school. I'm quiet, introspective. I know this is the last time this will happen. My body is broken, my heart is broken, and I know my home is broken as well. I'm bleeding, I'm wounded, I don't know what will happen, but I know that I have chosen myself. I have my children, and I have myself.

Tom calls obsessively throughout the day. I don't answer, not even once. Not a whore, but I do go to Noga—he was right about that. It's my first time seeing her after the abortion. I come to her with a trembling womb. And her bosom becomes a refuge for my head, my back, my breasts, my belly. I come to her bleeding, open. We make gentle, soft love, as much as I can, physically. I cry easily but don't tell her my relationship is falling apart. She embraces me. She doesn't ask for words, just listens to the pain in my heart and body. I'm careful with myself. When Tom and I are in a bad place and she is good, compassionate, and loving, when I lay my head on her stomach and she strokes my hair, when she looks into my eyes and understands everything without my having to say a word, it's dangerous for me. Dangerous to fall on her. Dangerous for her to be my savior. It's mine to hold. Mine to solve. Mine to break.

Tom is waiting for me at home. He looks terrible. He understands, finally understands, that the rules of the game have changed. He tells me he's made an appointment with a therapist. It is the first time in his life he's done so, made a decision to help himself. He swears everything will change. I ask him to stop making promises; I'm repulsed by his words. I agree to stay, willing to accept only actions from now on.

It's been one week since the extraction. I'm on the examination table again. Again the white bricks to my left. Vaginal ultrasound. This time I don't hold Tom's hand. I'm a badass and I don't need him anymore. He's there because I allowed it. The aborted children were his too, even though it occurred in me. The doctor frowns, identifying a large blood clot in my uterus. "It doesn't look good," he says. "If it doesn't come out—you'll have to be induced at the hospital."

He injects misoprostol into my uterus. Four 200 microgram tablets, 800 micrograms in total.

In the car on the way home, the contractions begin. I ask Tom to drive slowly, to be careful on the turns. By the time we arrive home, I'm in excruciating pain.

I lie in bed, bleeding, experiencing intense contractions but, instead of giving birth, I am birthing death. There are no consoling endorphins, no joy of life, only pain that splits me in two, cleaving the Great Rift Valley in my stomach.

I'm curled up on the bed, experiencing pitch-black agony that floods me with tears and desperation. The chasm of my life has opened, and I am diving in. I die with my twins and feel how alive I am through my body that is burning from the pain.

Another week passes with me staying in bed. Tom, the busy manager, takes care of the kids and the house all week. He makes fresh-squeezed orange juice for everyone in the mornings. Brings food to me in bed. I don't know what is happening outside the walls of my bedroom. The kids come in occasionally to burrow with me in bed. I don't know who is taking them to pre-school and school, who is bringing them home, what they're eating, whether they're brushing their teeth or not.

I bleed nonstop and, when I'm able to get out of bed, I go up to the roof to smoke. Tom and I communicate, utilitarian. He functions as he never has before. Chooses to be a father in this household. There is an abyss between us and there is a bridge, but it is high and shaky, and it depends on restraint. Conditional husband. The fucker is fucked.

Like a bear waking up from hibernation, my eyes open. Dragon fire shows up to help me. The bleeding women imprinted in my DNA, all the bleeding women ever, stand with me, shoulder to shoulder. Womb to womb. I'm as strong as an elephant and in the pit of my belly the dream is alive, as is its fracture.

Third week. Another check-up. The examination table again. Again the white bricks to my left, close and cold. Another ultrasound and again the doctor says, "No. The womb is still full of blood, we have to stop this."

He asks for my permission to do another extraction and again to give me misoprostol. As if I would say no. As if I have a choice. I appreciate the gesture and tell him "Sure, do whatever it takes." I already understand that this abortion has come to me straight from hell. I understand that my womb still hasn't given up on them. I'm not pregnant and they are no longer, but my womb is still searching for them, the children who were torn out of her.

Again the thick plastic syringe, again I fondle the brick to distract myself. It doesn't work. It hurts less than the first time. Again he inserts four misoprostol tablets, his gloved chubby fingers placing the capsules of the realm of the underworld inside me. Tom looks at me with tears in his eyes. He has cried a lot these past two weeks. I know it will be painful again, but this time I know there will be someone to take care of the house and the kids. This makes it easier for me.

Another week passes by in bed. Bleeding, cramps, death contractions. I am grieving. I'm weak and tired and I can't remember the last time I felt good, maybe a month and a half ago. Tom cooks for me for the first time in our life. He makes me a slow-cooked pot roast and, with every bite, I feel myself getting stronger, both from the iron and from the intention he puts in the meal. I'm still losing blood, still pale, still unsure about my life, my relationship, my direction, but I manage to hold myself. I'm aware of my environment. I start to get up a few times and I am steady standing on my two feet.

Fourth week since the abortion, another check-up at the doctor's. He says that I've broken all the statistics. Again I spread my legs on the examination table. Again Tom is behind me. Again those white bricks, which I will never, ever forget. Another ultrasound. The doctor sees what I already knew before we came. "Everything is fine," he says. The abortion is over. Four weeks of holocaust in my womb have come to an end. I close my legs, get dressed slowly and get off the examination table.

*Cunt*

*The most basic curse, you cunt*
*Who the fuck are you. What the fuck are you. Cunt. Motherfucker.*
*The lowest of the low. Total darkness.*
*The nothingness. The void. Fuck your motherfucking cunt.*

*Strong. Tough. Delicate. Sensitive.*
*It opens it gapes it's penetrated*
*It's deep it's wild it's miraculous*
*Cunt.*

*Protect your cunt*
*Fragile, desired, soft*
*Protect your cunt*
*So they won't slip into you penetrate you seduce you*

*They will take from you*
*Take You*
*Steal from you exploit you*
*Protect your cunt*

*And when it's right—your cunt will introduce you to paradise*
*You'll get closer to yourself and to it*
*And compassion and grace will arrive. Soft and encompassing*
*Passing the Divine Presence through your cunt.*

*And in birth, the cunt will split, go wild*
*Blaze and burn and stretch*
*The portal between creation and realization,*
*the connecting of soul to flesh*
*Is in your cunt.*

*The entire world through the cunt*
*Life. Mother of all living. Cunt*
*The very essence of your being. Dah.*

*The organ that cried and screamed your right to exist on earth*
*This holy organ that became a curse*
*Cunt*
*Bow down and thank it.*

# What Happens Behind Closed Doors

You open the door for me and immediately lock it behind me. We embrace, kiss, and my hand instinctively finds its way into your hair, starting from the nape of your neck. "I missed you so much," I murmur. I press you against the wall, firmly grasping your arms at your sides. I kiss you, tracing your lips and tongue with mine, pausing to gaze into your eyes before continuing. We kiss with fiery mouths, you pressed against the wall and against me.

I lift your arms above your head. A soft sigh escapes you, and I'm already so wet. You're wearing your grey dress and those high heels you love. You lift one leg, wrap it around me, the sharp edge of your heel digging into my calf, making me even wetter.

I kiss you deeply, lick you, bite along the length of your neck, one bite after another from your ear to your shoulder, all while holding your hands tightly. I lick your raised arms, moving from one to the other as you watch me, your mouth seeking mine until I return to it for a kiss.

I nip at your collarbone, then trace it with my tongue, tilting your chin up before finding your mouth again. We taste each other as if we are starving. I bite your ear, then grip you tightly, pinning your arms against the wall with one hand while the other roams free.

I crouch slightly, bringing my face level with your chest. Through the cotton of your dress, I take your tit into my mouth, feeling your nipple harden through the material. I massage your breast with my lips, still holding you firmly, listening to your groans. I am so wet, and I know you are too.

I rise again to your face level and, with my finger, push aside your panties and penetrate you, direct and confident. Your soft pink envelops me. My hand moves back and forth inside you, discovering the worlds within you, your storms, your beautiful heart pulsing around my hand. Our eyes lock. We're pressed tight against each other on the wall and I fuck you standing up, underneath your dress. Beneath the world's radar. Beneath criticism, propriety, how things should or shouldn't be.

My finger moves in and out of you. Our tongues intertwine, in your mouth in mine in ours. We sway to the music of our breaths and sighs, audible only to us. Goosebumps, flocks of geese passing through us. You're so wet, waterfalls of syrup flow over my finger. You cry out into my shoulder. Your scent intoxicates me. I continue fucking and gripping, breathing you in and out, listening to you roar. I could go on like this for hours, for days, until you push me away. Until your legs quiver. Until you throw me off, breathless, sweaty, spent and dripping.

I'll let you recover. And then I'll come to you again.

# Inferno

It's unbearable. The air between us is toxic. He feels I'm critical and unpleasant. I sense constant judgment from him and his dissatisfaction with me. I don't have enough kind words from him to hold on to. Birthday wishes once a year don't cut it. I do receive harsh words from him. Cutting. He doesn't hold back on those. He's open-hearted when spilling venomous words on me. I'm suffocating. I can't breathe. I have no beloved. No lover. No weed to dull the pain. Right now there are no cigarettes or alcohol or sugar because of the detox. Gallons of vomit, diarrhea. It's been years since this happened to me, as if cleansing Noga out of my system, purifying me of everything that was.

He ate my chocolate again (dark, 68% that my mother brought me from Prague). I told him with disappointment that there was no safe and secure place for my things in this house. He exploded at me. Yelled. Wouldn't stop. He berated me for ten minutes like a trans-Siberian train barreling through the belly of a mountain. God, how he hurt me because I complained about the chocolate, twice. He let the first time go. The second time I went too far, crossed his boundaries. The second time "drove him crazy," he said. He went berserk. Raised his voice so the kids heard.

Today he didn't curse. Didn't hurl his venom at me. Didn't slaughter me with his words. Today I was just "not okay," a bummer, critical, harsh.

I apologized.

He ate my chocolate (again and again he does this, deaf to my requests. To the boundaries I set). He yelled at me, and I'm the one who had to apologize. Then he said he's trying to ensure minimal interactions between us, so why do I have to make comments and pick at him.

That hurt more than anything. "Is that what you want?" I recoiled like a child who tried to hug a hungry jackal, mistaking it for a golden retriever. In my mind, I thought we were in this together. I thought we would grow closer. When he told me he wanted minimal interaction, I didn't know what stung more—that it was what he wanted, or that he said it because he wanted to hurt me.

I can't understand his love. When it's good, no one loves more fiercely than he does. He loves with a pure heart, in total devotion, with sweet words and honest passion. But when he's hurt, I become a dangerous enemy. His mouth transforms into a weapon of precise destruction. He won't stop until he sees me reduced to ashes.

My frustration wounds him. He sees me as critical, harsh. His constant refrain is: "you're unpleasant." How is it possible to live in such toxicity? His aggression and mine in this house, in my chest.

I made a conscious choice to be here. I decided this is what I want. That I love him and am in love with him (there are moments). That he is beautiful in my eyes and touches my heart. I put myself here. I tore myself away from her. From a warm bosom and endless acceptance. From softness and generosity, sweet lips, body worship, and constant joy at my presence and words. I severed that connection to truly be with him.

And then this. Whiplash. Always in reaction to me. It's always my fault. Always because I said something wrong. Not nice. Not the correct way. Not how it should be said. "You only react," he says. If only I were different, this wouldn't happen. If only I were pleasant, this wouldn't happen. It's true, if I were a sweet doll, this wouldn't happen. But I'm not.

So he lashes out. Wildly. The intensity of 200 pounds of anger leveraged against me. Crushes me with his words. With his tone. With the truth (or a slice of it), painful and direct. "Whatever you say to me—you'll get a thousand times in return." That's his motto. "So you learn. So you know not to speak to me like that."

When it's over, he forgets. Puts his hand on me because it's done. Why don't you let it go. Why can't you lighten up. Why can't you move past it. I've been trapped in this cycle for fifteen years.

I can't make a misstep because the price of my mistakes is devastating. And maybe I'm creating this. This is where the abused woman in me surfaces.

I relax when he bombards me with harsh words. I know I'll provoke him (I mean, I knew today that the chocolate comment wouldn't go over well, and still, I couldn't restrain myself. Like an itch I have to scratch. Why? Only bad can come of it. Bad, bad, came out). And yet. I provoke him. And then I blame myself. Know he'll blame me and there's no one else at fault, only my guilt.

As if his dragons are merely reacting to me. They lie dormant in my consciousness and when I step on their tail, they rise above me and begin to breathe fire (I don't believe this. I don't really believe it's my fault, the dragons).

When he spits his black smoke at me, I get that choking feeling in my chest. The pressure closes in on me. I curl up into myself like a fetus. Collect anew the parts of my body. Murmur inside to myself, swear to get revenge. To love another woman. To open a separate bank account. Not to love him like I know that I know how to love.

And then it passes for him. "I love you." He goes back to life as usual. The dragons go back to sleep.

For me, my belly burns. Without the weed, I forget more

slowly. Really feel my trampled heart. Don't know how to escape this except to wait for forgetfulness. It always comes. I always forget and move on, because life. It's impossible to sit in stagnant, fetid waters. I transfer the water, flush this existential toilet. Move forward.

Again, with time, I fall in love with his eyes. With his chest muscles. His voice. The cruel words become dull and I'm a sweet doll, until the next time.

# Constructive Change

I arrive at "Build and Renew Engineering Inc." filled with excitement.

For years, I've worked underneath, above, and alongside greed. Now, wearing tailored pants and a button-down shirt, I stroll through the main entrance of the management building of one of the country's largest engineering companies. Build and Renew Engineering is a corporation with thousands of employees and projects worldwide: power plants, desalination facilities, toll roads.

I was accepted into the Concessions Department after a rigorous process involving interviews with professional and management teams, aptitude tests, and security clearance. "This entire massive ship sails according to the direction of the tenders you win," the CEO lectured us during a departmental team-building day. I admit, it worked. I was filled with motivation and a sense that I was part of something big and significant.

I had never worked such an institutional job before. Although we were defined as an elite unit ("you are the company's crown jewels," they'd repeatedly toast at meetings—apparently, there's always a need to polish the family jewels in the manly mantras mythologized by the males in charge), but there was still a time-card to stamp and department-wide meetings. There was a staff, a schedule, a shared calendar, habits, a dress code, norms.

"How are you going to handle it, at a corporation?" Tom asked me, knowing what kind of person he had married.

"I'll handle it," I answered simply, "because it's what I want right now."

I wanted to experiment with the clean-cut, straight world. I wanted stability, I wanted to take part in the movement of something being built from nothing and, mostly, I wanted to make a difference from within. I thought that with my very presence I could change something of the organizational, patriarchy-weary culture.

My job was as a project manager for tenders. Around two hundred people from seven countries around the world worked on each tender. I sat in the center of the web and made sure that all the spiders did their jobs and that all of their output was up to the tender's demands. I alerted about possible problems popping up, spoke with dozens of people a day, made sure that all the strands of the web connected to each other. The deadline for each tender was a year out. There was no room for error. From the moment the tender was made public, we hit the ground running, building an offer that was economically smart, legally admissible and structurally sound.

For the first few months I was entertained by how things worked, afterward I wondered and, finally, I was shook. These were the people laying our national infrastructural foundations? These are the people we should trust? I wouldn't let them caulk the shower in my bathroom, let alone build a country.

One of the team members, Benny, a lawyer by profession who had been ejected from the legal firms where he had done his internship, found himself at the engineering company and blossomed there. Benny, more than anything, loved to talk about himself. He was the first to arrive in the morning and the last to leave at night. He would brag to us about working into the early hours of the morning and on weekends. To me that was only evidence of his inefficiency, but hey, what do I and research from Harvard know? Maybe 20-hour workdays really are the path to happiness.

"Did you hear the news?" Benny once said to me as the elevator doors opened. I was just going up from the parking lot to the fourth floor, where the offices for the jewels were. I was a bit startled when he jumped in front of the elevator doors. "They announced that I'm the project manager for the new freeway interchange at Barley Hills."

"Great, great," I replied, my hair still damp from the sea. On days with good waves, I'd shower at the beach after my session, change clothes in the car, and apply my makeup at red lights.

"I'm a genius," Benny would mutter to himself in the hallways, and I'd shake my head, feeling as if I were in an asylum for the intellectually stunted. He'd prowl the corridors, seeking out other men to regale with his tedious tales—how he'd cracked the maintenance model issue with a contractor, or how the guys in the Energy Division didn't understand a thing. His voice carried so loudly that I could hear his conversations through the plaster walls of my office.

"So how are your boys?" Benny would ask me when he yearned for small talk, and I couldn't slip out of his eyesight.

"I have one son," I answered him, "and two daughters."

"Oh, right, right,"

I walked those hallways as if no woman had ever stepped foot there before. Yes, there were a few women, but most of them were secretaries. The company's legal team was headed by a formidable, impressive woman, with brilliant female lawyers working under her. But in the other departments, it was just me and men in button-down shirts. Starched shirts and faded shirts, shirts straining over protruding bellies and shirts revealing sinewy arms. Dozens, hundreds of men. And me.

I strode through, tan and in dresses. I walked around after nights of mind-blowing orgasms while managing a personal double-life. I balanced raw passion and pragmatic existence in ways they could never fathom.

"So how was it on the SUP?" Benny would ask me.
"I surf waves," I answered.
"Oh, right, right."

An engineer named Slava would sneak into my office and leave surprises on my desk. He'd construct miniature sculptures from objects he found in the room. Once, he balanced a green apple on my computer screen, topped with a ChapStick, with a pile of staples perched on top. Another time, he propped two notebooks against each other, placed a bottle nearby, and balanced a pen across them like a bridge. I found it charming, in a geeky sort of way.

Every day, I'd snap a picture of his latest creation and send it to Noga. She didn't share my amusement. "It's creepy," she said, "the man doesn't respect boundaries." When I found my earbuds jammed into a gum container, I realized she was right. I confronted him, and that was the last time he left his surprises on my desk.

Sometimes I'd encounter the men in the office in the morning, and I could tell they'd masturbated over me the night before. I recognized the look in their eyes. They'd smile at me sheepishly, as if we'd shared an intimate night together. Only in your dreams, tiara, only in your dreams.

Damien was cut from a different cloth entirely. An enormous man, tall and fat, with the eternal smile of a good-natured bear. He'd fish a toothpick from his shirt pocket and pick at his teeth during meetings, whether in person or over Zoom. For countless calls, I had to watch his quivering double chin because he never mastered the art of angling his camera. He'd join video calls from his car while driving, that ever-present toothpick working between his teeth.

This wasn't my main issue with him though.

Damien didn't suffer from imposter syndrome, unfortunately. He wasn't an employee of the company, but rather served as a specialist external consultant and received an exorbitant salary. I knew this because I had access to all the employment contracts in the department. He'd tell us all about his elderly mother and how, since she'd lost her memory, he helped her settle into a new nursing home. He'd share stories about his swimmer daughter's shoulder injury and the surgery she'd soon undergo. With his affable personality, he wormed his way into people's hearts, encouraging them to share their own life challenges in return.

This mountain of a man would initiate hallway conversations with everyone, from the CEO to the parking lot guard, with great cordiality. He remembered details, names, dates, and made a point of asking and showing interest. That way, when he needed something—be it professional information about railroads or crane types, a VIP's phone number, or juicy gossip about an employee—he'd tug at the thread he'd carefully placed, pulling and pulling until he unraveled the stubbornness or ethics on the other end and got what he was after. And then, at the opportune moment, he'd present the information as if it were his own. Unlike Benny, Damien truly was a genius.

"I can't believe these are the people managing billion-dollar projects," I said to Tom. "No wonder our planet looks the way it does." I was always learning—not just about tender submission stages, engineering, and project management, but about the secrets of the corporate ego.

Every Thursday at four, we'd gather in the department lobby for a toast. It was always whiskey or ouzo, brought back from duty-free by one of the employees. Benny kept the bottles in his office, very proud of his role, pouring the spirit of choice into tiny plastic cups. Sometimes Rivkal'eh, the department secretary, would set out fruit or cookies before joining us for a quick glass and then hurrying home.

Our most important staff meeting of the week followed at five.

At first, I was surprised they'd chosen Thursday evening, of all times. I knew the chaos of late afternoons at home with kids: homework, showers, fights, lice checks, wet towels, the dog wants to go out, scrambled eggs, vegetables. Yet there we were, seated around the wooden table in the conference room, a representative from each tender present. Some nursed coffee cups. Two water carafes stood on the table, flanked by stacks of plastic cups. Someone opened the windows to ward off shared viruses. Some sat with a notebook and pen next to them, some with a laptop.

By then, the building had emptied save for us, the crown jewels, and the guards.

The men spoke in loud, confident voices, joking around, trading quips. Every professional statement carried a tone of self-importance, but they smiled even as they said things like, "That's bullshit," or "Let me explain why you're wrong."

Of course they're smiling, I thought to myself. They don't have to convince their kid to come home from the playground while she shouts that she hasn't gone down the slide enough times yet today. They don't have to pick bell pepper off the floor while their kid yells that his sister snatched his sandwich off his plate.

We would finish the meeting at seven in the evening and only then head down to the parking lot, each of us driving home slowly through the weekend traffic. By the time I got home, the babysitter had already settled the children into their pajamas and the house was quiet. Then I understood why the most important meeting took place on Thursday at five.

I remember one meeting in particular. Marcelo showed everyone a picture of his daughter in her ballet outfit. He told a funny story about her, how she dances however she wants, unrelated to what the rest of her dance troupe is doing.

"She's adorable," they told him.

"Why aren't you with your daughter at this hour instead of

sitting here with us, showing us pictures of her?" I didn't ask him.

I grew accustomed to the deep, low masculine voices. My voice was high and small, true woman, a biological success. I could never beat them on their home turf. If I tried to speak at the same time as they did, their voices would steamroll mine and my words would be swallowed. So over the years, I developed tactics.

I wait for a moment of quiet and then I jump in with my words. Dana and I call it 'threading.' I need to do it quickly and precisely, deliver a concentrated sentence at the right moment, thwack. Thread the information in like an epidural straight into the spine of the lively conversation.

Sometimes it doesn't work, like the time I gambled incorrectly on the timing and there wasn't a vocal pause in their chorus of bass. I said: "Let's think about generating renewable energy for the project, maybe solar panels on the facility's roof," but the men's commotion swallowed my voice.

I waited for the next opportunity to thread myself in, and then Damien thundered in his bear-like voice: "We need to include renewable energy in the project, for example solar panels on the roof." When I looked at him, astonished, he stared straight into my eyes, didn't even blink.

"There's no denying it, that Damien knows what he's doing," I told Dana.

"Worth his weight in gold," she replied.

I found my own ways to express myself. I wrote clear emails. I created warm relationships with each and every one of my team members, all around the world. Sometimes I managed to thread the needle, sometimes I didn't, but I felt I was making some kind of change. My team was relaxed, we worked collaboratively rather than competitively. My maternal efficiency trumped their complaints about the odd hours I punched on my time-card, about my excessive care in using gender-inclusive language.

"Where were you this morning?" Yuval, the CEO, asked me once.

"What do you mean?" I answered. There were waves this morning.

"I went past your office at nine-thirty and you weren't there."

I'm over forty and I haven't followed orders for a while. I provided the company with project management that combined determination with gentleness. I demanded excellence from my team, and I also empowered and complimented them. Years as a mother trained me to juggle multi-tasking with the same skill that Benny practiced unjustified self-aggrandizement. He thinks he's going to tell me what time to come in? I thought. Oh, poor, confused Yuvali.

"I don't understand the problem," I replied. "The engineering staff meeting starts at 11, and I already signed the consultant's statements yesterday. Vanessa from legal is checking about the Spanish veto rights, and Tony sent two sketches of the tunnel. You can see the update in the Gantt chart I sent last night."

"Yes, I understand," he said and didn't understand. "But it doesn't look good, Elinor. Everyone gets here at eight, nine at the latest. People raise an eyebrow when you come in late. I ask that it not happen again."

"Okay," I answered and thought to myself: What's good is that you know how to ask, it's important to know how to ask. How is it not funny to him? I wondered. He's so serious and solemn in this conversation, confused between output and clock hands, between efficiency and appearances.

Three days later there were waves again and again I arrived late to the office, this time at ten. Again he called me in for exactly the same conversation. Again I said: "Okay."

Build and Renew Engineering once published a job ad for a

manager of activities in Romania, addressed only to men in its language. They sent it to the newspapers and also in the organizational email to everyone in the company. I reached out to the head of the international division and his assistants. "If we have a female Israeli ambassador to Romania, and a woman economic attaché in Romania, you can address the ad to all genders, including women," I told them.

"You're right," they replied and slightly changed the language in the ad. "Nuisance," they probably thought to themselves. "Misogynists," I thought back at them. It was a man, of course, who was chosen for the position.

# Interchange

I was with Noga for five years, parallel to my marriage. On his part, mine chose to ignore our polyamory, donning a blindfold as he galloped down a seemingly heteronormative life path. I loved him; I didn't give up. Her husband also accepted us, overlooking, agreeing, turning a blind eye. We existed in a square containing three couples: the two of us, the two of them, and she and I.

As the children grew older, I resumed my ambitious career trajectory, the one I was on before Lev was born. I kept my promise to myself not to return to corporate espionage. Instead, I worked on desalination plants, train lines, and interchanges. They called them mega-projects. The demands were high, but so was the salary. I spent many hours in traffic, commuting back and forth.

We were both busy but made sure to meet once a week, between her house and mine, between her life and mine. Once a week, I was hers. I wanted more and asked her for it. She'd reply, "I'm so with you, I think about you all the time," yet refused to meet more frequently. Between her children and job, it wasn't possible for her. "I want to," she'd say, "but I can't."

"She's stringing you along," Dana said to me. "She's stingy and you're settling for crumbs."

"But she's always so generous," I countered. "She always listens to me, holds space for me, she's so gentle." I tried to reconcile the contradiction within myself.

'Wants to but can't'—what a strange combination of words.

I believed that Noga believed it, but I stopped accepting it as a valid stance. "A woman desires—a woman does," Dana's words echoed in my mind. "Doesn't desire—doesn't do."

When the COVID-19 pandemic broke out, Noga and I, like everyone else, stopped seeing each other. I could move around easily because the infrastructure sector was deemed 'essential work,' and I had a signed authorization from my job. I drove back and forth to the corporate offices on ghostly empty highways, presenting my permit at every police checkpoint along the way.

In my eagerness, I suggested visiting Noga in her town. "Whenever you say, whenever you want," I told her—or rather, pleaded with her. I longed to be with her for an hour, two hours, a night, whatever she would agree to. She refused.

She feared infection or exposure, or perhaps she didn't know how to explain such a meeting to her husband. No matter how hard I tried, I couldn't get to the bottom of her sweeping, stubborn refusal.

During one of the lulls between lockdowns, Noga told me that her children were hosting other kids from the neighborhood at their house. "There must be like ten kids here right now!" she said proudly, perhaps trying to impress me with her capacious parenting skills. They usually did impress me, but not this time.

It was the straw that broke the groaning she-camel's back. 'Seriously? You're hosting kids but won't invite me to see you?' I didn't say aloud but thought. My heart shriveled and bounced around in my gut.

After the brief respite, lockdowns closed in on us again and my heart, too, began to close off to her.

Dana had been a member of a polyamorous dating group on Facebook for years. She noticed a post from someone who piqued her interest. "You should meet her, give it a try," she told me. "What do you have to lose?"

"Noga," I answered.

"You can't lose something you've already lost," Dana said, her words sharp as ever.

I read the message Dana forwarded to me.

The woman described herself as a lesbian, a feminist, a womanist. She wrote that she was sexual, passionate, curious. To me, she seemed like a social butterfly, flitting from country to country, from woman to woman. She stated that she wasn't looking for commitment and didn't want exclusivity. It sounded perfect to me.

"Alright," I told Dana, "introduce us."

Second Portal

**MOWGLI**
2020

# Womanist

I arrived at her place looking corporate: tailored pants, a white button-down shirt and black leather heels. My eyes were rimmed with black eyeliner, my hair pulled back into a high, tight ponytail—the way I prefer it at the office, keeping it out of my face. We sat on her porch beneath a pergola, sipping tea she'd brewed from her own herb garden, and we talked. She wore loose burgundy harem pants and a snug brown tank top, a thin woman with a mass of big curls. An Aladdin-a who'd washed up on a kibbutz in the midst of her world travels.

"I'm a womanist," she declared. "Queer, non-hierarchical polyamorous, a switcher." She had a label for everything. Her dimples charmed me; she was cute and easy-going. She made me laugh, asked a lot of questions, and listened intently to my answers. She's one of those people who genuinely cares, I thought to myself. How rare.

Her skin was bronzed from the two years she'd spent in South America. "I'm a born nomad," she told me, "I came into this world with a Bedouin soul." Every few months, she'd pack up her meager possessions and move on to the next destination. A forty-year-old Peter Pan. Brazil. Peru. Colombia. Never-Never Land.

She had landed in Israel with the outbreak of the coronavirus and rented a small unit on her parents' kibbutz. When the worst was over, she would flit away again. It made things clear. She was a passerby, and that was perfect for me—for me and for Tom, who didn't like sharing me but agreed because otherwise I would slip through his fingers.

After a three-hour conversation on her balcony, she walked me to my car and we hugged. The embrace was warm, full-bodied, and lasted far longer than the obligatory second. When it ended, she said: "Come again. I want you to."

We texted for hours, for days, trying to find the right time to meet again. She wrote: "Goddess, I want you in my bed. It will take a while, not an hour, not two or three, so make time."

"I met someone," I told Noga during a phone call. We hadn't seen each other in four months but still texted, sometimes spoke on the phone. She kept talking, then suddenly stopped. "Wait, what did you say?"

"I met someone I'm interested in."

"Elinor," she said.

"Yes."

"No."

"Sweetie."

"If you're telling me this, it means it's already happening."

"Nothing has happened yet, but she interests me. I want to explore it."

"I want to end this conversation," she said. "I'll talk to you later. I need to be alone right now."

Noga's wise expansiveness had saved me. Her pale legs had rescued me from the dark abyss in my marriage. Everything had fractured there with the abortion. My belly, my uterus, my trust in him—all shattered. With her soft feminine power, her gentle and attentive listening, she had nursed me back to life.

Her eyes, full of belief in me, drew me out towards the light. She supported me when I was offered a job at the engineering firm. When they promised me engagement, excitement, and growth. National infrastructure, mega-projects. She saw me as a mega-woman. She had saved me.

Later that night, Noga wrote to me: "It's me or her, Elinor.

I can handle Tom, that's the deal, that's always been the deal. But another woman—it's too much for me."

"I'm sorry," I wrote back. "I love your pure, sweet heart. I really don't want to hurt you, but there are parts of me seeking to be realized."

"Then it's over between us," she concluded. "Good luck."

I sent her a red heart in response. It was the last time we communicated.

# Mowgli

Here I am again, at the kibbutz gate. She opens it for me, and the yellow barrier slides open to the left at a snail's pace, in stark contrast to my mounting excitement. I remember the way, park, and walk down the quiet kibbutz path to her place. I've brought flowers—how romantic of me—medicinal cannabis buds I bought from a friend whose father has Parkinson's. She opens the door, and I'm drawn into her warm embrace. I laugh, embarrassed and excited.

She brews us tea from her garden herbs—sage, verbena—with plenty of honey, and we sit on a mattress in the living room. She rolls us a joint, which turns out pleasantly plump. We talk and pass it between us. She's participated in tantra workshops, learned sacred sexuality. Again, she lists her definitions: non-hierarchical polyamorous, multi-orgasmic, anarchist, free spirit. She studies me, and I feel shy like a girl on a first date with a graduate student.

Next to her, I feel so conventional. As if I've dragged the bourgeois lifestyle, the kids, and the corporate job with me to the kibbutz. I'm married-at-first-sight giddy.

She calls me from where she's sitting on the mattress, "Come here." I move closer, and we position ourselves cross-legged, facing each other. She begins to stroke my arms, and I reciprocate, hazy from the joint and her chocolate presence. I feel like she's examining me with wise, 90-year-old eyes. I'm passive, which is odd for me and thrilling all at once.

The caressing continues with music playing in the background, and I move as if I'm dancing. It calms me, connecting me to the here and now. She senses my excitement and reassures me that it's okay, that everything will be at my pace. "We have all night," she says. I correct her—not exactly all night. Sunrise is at five, and I want to be home when the kids wake up. "Okay," she smiles, "half the night."

I ask her permission to remove the shirt she's wearing—if you can call a single-buttoned fabric a shirt. She invites me to do so. I play with her scarf, twining it around my fingers before winding it around her neck. It's pleasant, soft, beige-hued wool. I roll down the fabric of her shirt, revealing sun-kissed shoulders. I lean in to kiss them, yearning to know her through my lips.

I'm overwhelmed by her strong scent. She says it's coconut oil that she spreads over her entire body every day, but to me it smells like eucalyptus. She's strong; I bite-kiss her. She requests that the bites be quick. I'm overly self-conscious, feeling like I'm trying too hard and struggling to be in the moment. It's a delicate balance, and I'm stoned and very excited. I feel like I'm failing, but I don't stop trying. I insist, coming back to the here and now. She sighs with her neck raised; I understand that she's enjoying herself.

We separate to remove my shirt. It's a big black t-shirt; underneath, a bra. I was too embarrassed not to wear one, as if it wasn't clear to both of us that I came to get undressed. I take off my shirt and then my bra, and sit before her with my upper body nude. I lie back so she can see me. As I am, with my body that gave birth to three children, with my drooping breasts and my stomach that had been ripped apart by pregnancies. My shoulders are strong from the sea, and my hair is long and black, and it is what it is. I feel beautiful in her gaze. I feel like a woman. I look at her and she looks at me. She smiles.

She brings her mouth close to mine but doesn't kiss. We smell each other. My lips touch her cheeks, our cheeks brush against each other. I inhale her scent deeply. Eucalyptus and coconut and two years in the sun. How wild this woman is, a deserted island in the middle of the ocean.

We smile at each other. I hold her scarf and pull her to me. We don't kiss yet. She has big lips and horse-like teeth. I love it.

I'm frustrated; I so want her mouth and she's teasing me, getting closer and then further away. My pussy is awake; she leaves me yearning.

All at once she inhales and then dives straight into my lips. With quick, sure movements, she takes me for a trip in her mouth. My diving instructor, I'll follow her wherever she goes.

We kiss and caress each other. Music plays in the background from the laptop beside us. Suddenly, a realization hits me. "You're Mowgli, the jungle boy!" I exclaim, and she erupts in strong, liberating laughter. Her laugh reminds me of my friend Moran, a musician in New York. She, too, has curly hair and dark skin, with a profound beauty that reveals itself on second and third glances. I'm delighted to have made her laugh.

She tells me no one has ever said that to her before. "Wow, what a compliment," she adds. I'm proud. I mark this moment in my mind. I'm seen. I matter. This is so basic for me.

She leans over to kiss my tits, and I recline, stretching for her. I present my body like a puppy at a dog-show. I want to be beautiful in her eyes. She sucks my breasts, massages my nipples with her tongue, licks around the areolas. I moan.

She cups my breasts and asks, "How do you like your tits to be touched?"

I echo, "What?" not because I didn't hear her, but to buy time to think. The answer is complex. It depends on when and who, and maybe I'm still learning what I like. But I'm out of time; I need to be communicative and answer. She squeezes my breasts, hard. So I say, "Hard."

She kisses me and grabs my breasts firmly. Currents of pain

and pleasure intertwine like strands of DNA, climbing up my body. I'm hot. My pussy begins to move toward her as her hips move toward me.

We sit facing each other and she grabs my hair, pulling it back hard while simultaneously moving her hips with precision and depth. She lifts me to sit on her, and I comply. We're both still in pants, topless. Our legs are spread, pussy to pussy, and she moves me against her in ways I've never experienced before. She moves like a man with a cock, determined, but I've never slept with any man who was like this. It's unlike anything I know.

Her scent is intense and overwhelms my nostrils. She makes noises, takes deep breaths, and my heart rate goes wild. My pussy is raging for her under my pants and underwear; the energy she's passing to me makes me lose my mind. I release my hips and let her dictate the rhythm. She pumps me against her in skillful fucking movements, one hand holding my hair and the other wreaking havoc on my breast.

I hold onto her shoulders. They're narrow. It's strange for me; I'm used to riding Tom and gripping his broad shoulders. She's not like Tom and not like Noga. My tits send electric signals and my mind becomes cloudy.

"There's a rule," she says. "No coming." Okay, I think, I can do that.

She continues with the fucking motions, breathing heavily, then suddenly stops. No coming.

"Come to the bedroom," she tells me.

"Yes!"

We disconnect from each other but, instead of standing up, I pounce on her with embarrassing lack of self-control. I lay her back on the mattress, her head falling off the edge. In front of us, the laptop is open to a Microsoft screensaver image of a giant orange and black butterfly, a royal damselfly.

I lick her neck and sense the butterfly thirty centimeters away from us, glowing at me with digital light, reminding me exactly who I'm with. I stop licking, and we both stand up. She takes my hand and leads me to the bedroom.

## Squash

He comes home from a meeting as I'm cooking. Tailored pants, blue striped shirt. Men—why do they always wear blue? Like little kids, boys in blue or gray, while girls are in colors. He's lost weight, shed the belly that bothered me. Started running, going into the sea. His chest muscles press against his shirt. Sometimes I can look at him as if we'd just met, despite all the years and changes. It's the same spark in his eyes, that of a crazy prophet, that still does it for me.

He places his hand on my back. We exchange a few words about the new dresser and Michaela's basketball practice—it's our turn to carpool tomorrow. The conversation is pleasant, the tones soft. His hand returns to my back, sliding down to my ass.

"I would sleep with you right now," he says, as if testing my responsiveness.

"Is that an offer?" I ask.

He considers for a moment. "Yes, it's an offer."

I think as well. We smile at each other. I calculate in my head: in an hour I have to get the kids, I just put the food on the stove, the squash needs time to soften. So do I. Maybe the intimacy will drain the pain, or maybe it will emphasize how far apart we've grown. I'm willing to take the risk, to complicate things, to heal. I want to see how it will feel today.

"I want to," I tell him. "Let me finish here."

"I'll be waiting for you in bed," he says as he unbuttons his shirt.

The tofu is already in the pot. I add parsley, ginger, and water, then leave it on a low flame. When I reach the bedroom, I see him gargling with mouthwash.

"I smoked a cigarette," he explains.

I smile at him. "You don't need to explain."

We undress ourselves—the practicality of married life. We slip into bed in the middle of the afternoon; it's hot outside and our hearts are beginning to thaw. I lie on my back, legs open. He's above me on all fours, sporting a nice erection, caressing my body. He strokes my legs, my thighs, my shoulders, my arms. His touch is gentle and sweet, my body shudders and relaxes for him.

"I love you," he says, and his voice is home. "I want the best for you. Sometimes it's hard for me to accept all of this."

"I know," I tell him. "I love you too." I stroke his neck, hold his stubbled face. Being with him here feels like floating on a raft.

He slips just the tip of his cock into me and we keep talking. About us. About her. He continues caressing me, spending time on my legs. I concentrate on the conversation. On my pussy. On the conversation. On my pussy. "When things are good between us, I can take everything," he says.

"I know. This kind of openness is possible," I tell him, and I do open, becoming wet in new layers within me, which his cock enters slowly. He turns me on my side, my lower leg straight and my upper leg folded so that my entire thigh and side of my ass face him. I'm in a delightful twist, already open to receive all of him. But he doesn't give it yet.

He caresses my waist. He holds my stomach, strong from the sun and sea, weak from three children. He cradles my wild and broken belly in his large hand, and warmth spreads from my belly to my pussy. I'm completely wet now, moving my hips toward him, but he stops me. He remains with half his cock inside me, teasing my pleading body. His self-control makes me even wetter.

"You're so beautiful," he says, turning me a little more. Now I'm lying on my stomach, cheek pressed against the bed, as he penetrates me deeply. A grunt escapes me. He finds his rhythm, fucking me, and I feel ants crawling inside, from my vagina throughout my entire body, traveling through my veins. He grabs my hips and lifts me up. I rise to all fours with him behind me, the position that always pulls lion sounds from my throat. He grips my hips hard. His dick is so deep inside me, bordering on painful, but not. He bends forward and bites the nape of my neck, sending chills through my body. Fucking and biting. Fucking and gripping.

I want to keep going like this, on and on, forever, but he stops. He sits up straight in the middle of the bed and says, "Come to me." I straddle him, facing him. My legs are open and his cock slips into me. We sit in the middle of the bed, embracing, not moving. His cock is enveloped in me, and we pause time and movement in our embrace. I inhale his scent. He listens to my heart. For a moment, we are a capsule of quiet.

I start riding his dick. I take him so deep that the root of his cock presses against my pussy, then rise again. I pump up and down on him, focusing on his chest hair, where there are already a few white strands, his broad shoulders, his erect dick at the center of my body.

I lean back. My legs still spread for him, I'm on my elbows. We move towards each other, eyes locked as his dick slides in and out of me. I feel his balls slapping against my ass and, in sync with them, my breasts dance.

I lie all the way back and lift my legs to either side; he rises above me and starts fucking at an escalating pace. He pumps into me, and I moan. He thrusts in and out, determined and focused. His shoulders gleam with sweat, his muscles bulging, drops of perspiration falling from his face onto me. I stop him to get on top again and, in a second, I feel the orgasm building, a scream rising in my throat. I'm on the edge, I leap. I come, done, and he, he comes with me.

This orgasm brings tears. I cry into his shoulder. Cry from relief. From pain. From releasing the knot I didn't know was lodged in the center of my chest. "Thank you for agreeing to walk this path with me" I tell him. "I needed to hear that."

"I agree," he says. "I'm scared, and I agree."

We are two children holding hands in the bodies of adults who just finished fucking. No wonder I'm confused. The multitude of people who are here with us.

I return to the squash, which is now soft, tender. My pussy is sweet and my mind is quiet. I add coconut milk and watch the stew bubble. Still naked, I taste it and turn off the heat.

## Woman Steak in Coconut Oil

I arrive at the pathway in the kibbutz. I climb the five wooden steps to her balcony, open the screen door, and knock. She calls from inside: "Come in."

I open the door and see her in the corner. She's completely naked, sitting cross-legged before her altar, a kind of spiritual temple she created with incense, precious stones, and personal empowerment texts. She glistens with coconut oil she's lathered on herself. Behind her, a coil heater glows like an urban bonfire within four walls. I slip off my shoes in the entryway and approach her, drawn to the scent of coconut and freedom. Her body is warm and mine is cold; I'm careful not to touch her with my hands. I lay my longing neck against hers, breathe her in, and we stay like this, breathing gently.

She gets up to dress (what a shame) and makes us tea. We sit on the mattress in the living room and catch up. I tell her about work; she tells me about the new apartment she's moving to soon, still within the kibbutz. This will be our last time in this apartment. "Then let's celebrate," I tell her. We move to the bedroom, bringing the coil heater and our tea. Our tops fly off on the way. A few minutes later—our bottoms as well.

We sit upright in the middle of the bed. I straddle her and look across at our reflection in the mirror. I look at her boyish back, her wild curls, our four open thighs. Hers, mine, hers, mine. My hair forms a black halo around us. Her hand is already deep inside me; God, the things she does with that hand. I just got here, I think, but I'm wet and drawn to her, so I realize I arrived so ready.

I ride her hand, she feels my swirls and whispers to me "yes yes yes yes yes," and I am electrified, inhaling her edible scent deep within me. I suck her hand into me, feeling like I want to swallow all of her. We twist around each other as if a huge snake is coiling us together.

I lean back and she continues fucking me with her hand. She lifts me up so that I'm sitting on her pelvis. She's so skillful, my pussy whisperer, so gifted at talking to my pussy—that all I can do is surrender entirely. I open my dams to her, beginning to ooze and drip and bless us with my warm waters.

"I want to merge into you, to crawl under your skin," she tells me.

"That's exactly what you're doing," I reply.

I move closer and bite her neck, bite all the way from her shoulder to her neck, to her ears. My teeth make tracks along the outline of her upper body. She moans. Holds her breath. It feels good to her and that drives me crazy.

I need her back. "Lie on your stomach," I tell her. She does. Her tan ass is in front of my face and I can't do anything but kiss it. It's solid and soft exactly the way I like it. I'm a lustful bear, kissing and licking her honey-ass.

Her back calls to me. It's strong, sketched. She has a scrape between her shoulder blades from the last time we fucked and she was up against the wall. I'm careful. I kiss her back slowly, bite every once in a while.

"Hard," she asks, "harder." I'm hot, sitting with my legs spread wide over her ass, moving my hips on her.

I bite the back of her neck and she groans. "You're so wet," she tells me, feeling me wetting her ass. I twist on her and bite her, a starved lioness. Biting and biting her meat, a woman steak in coconut oil.

"You're so good," she says, "You're driving me crazy." I growl into her, continue biting and sucking her skin.

I pin her to the bed with my arms. We both have strong arms, I don't let her rise up. I want to fuck her hard, to devour the evil beasts within her, to trap them in the tangle of my womb.

I'm behind her, holding her tight against me, my hand grasping her neck. She guides me: "The thing is to regulate your intensity. You're strong, so pay attention. It's dangerous. I trust you." I kiss her lightly on the neck and then grip, hard. Stopping her breath.

My hips move against her in fucking motions, one hand clenched around her neck, controlling her very breath. With my other hand, I clutch the sheet in a tight fist. My pussy drips onto her ass and I make an effort not to come.

I'm walking a tightrope, striding over the gap between my desire to totally go wild on her, to let loose, and guarding her from me. I didn't know I could feel this way. To be simultaneously both the tamer and the lion, the dragon and the knight. With one hand still on her neck, I reach for her nipple and pinch it tightly between two fingers. Slowly I increase the pressure on her neck. Slowly I increase the pressure on her nipple. "Yes!" she squirms, she's coming! And coming and coming.

I wait until the storm subsides and then gradually release my grip. On her, on logic, on everything I've known or will know. I'm nothing, emptiness, and a divine spark from above. Slowly I lie down next to her. "God, wow."

"Yeah," she says, "wow."

I roll us a joint and she pets me in the meantime. My clitoris is swollen, my mouth is hot. Her back is covered in bite marks.

The flowers she put in a vase next to the bed cast shadows on the wall, and we pass the joint between us. The bed is warm, a big girls' playground. My heart is calm and my body awake and softened in a combination I've not known before. The joint passes between us like a tiny torch, altering the consciousness of two spirit-whirled beings.

# Cupping Therapy

My back aches with tension. It's no wonder—like every mother I know, I carry the weight of the world on my shoulders. I ask Tom to do some cupping therapy. We received a set as a gift from an acupuncturist friend, and they always help. In the bedroom, I peel off my shirt with slow movements and lie on my stomach in the center of the bed. Tom says, "First, we need to warm you up."

He begins to caress my back, then gently removes my pants and underwear. His hands glide over my ass, my legs, my back—ass, legs, back—in a sensual rhythm. The blood in my veins turns to warm butter.

He spreads me open and penetrates me slowly. With his cock barely inside, he pauses and begins massaging my back. His movements are smooth, panther-like. He stops at every knot of pain, feeling them, warming them. He pushes in a bit deeper, then resumes the massage. The stiffness in my back persists, the world still weighs upon it, but now Tom shares the burden. My chest feels lighter.

He penetrates further, pausing again to trail his long fingers along my skin. The tips of his fingers tell me: I see you. I see how hard it is. You're not alone. I breathe more and more deeply.

He penetrates deeper until his cock is fully inside me. He moves within me slowly, so slowly, and I grow wetter and wetter. Then he stops. His cock remains inside me, motionless, as he massages me thoroughly with his hands and places the first cup on my back, right at the center of the pain. He draws out the air with the pump. I hear the sound of suction, feel the vacuum pressing on my sore muscle, and he is there, filling me.

I try to move, but he stills me with his hand. He wants me completely passive. He fucks. Stops. Takes another cup from the box. Sets it next to the first one. Yes, there.

The sound of air being sucked out, a strong feeling of pulling. And he fucks.

Each time I attempt to move, he halts me, pressing his hand against my skin. Eventually, I yield. He fucks me more, and I grow wetter. Strong pressure on my back, as if twin lions are sinking their teeth into my flesh. His cock slides in and out of me, then he pauses to set another cup. And another. Four cups now pull at my back, biting into the pain. Stinging currents carve ravines through my body from my back. The wetness in my pussy meets them. Tom is inside me. Pain and pleasure intermingle in my legs, my pussy, my back, my arms, my head.

Tom withdraws and lies behind me on his stomach, his head between my legs. Wetness flows inside me, caressing the pain. I don't lift my pelvis, but his tongue easily finds my clitoris. He licks and licks, and I remain still. All the fire inside moves within my body. Externally, there's no movement; only I feel the ceaseless pull in the bonfire of pain at the center of my back. I'm hot. I'm burning. I'm melting. I'm a flying dragon. I soar over rivers and cliffs. Abundance unfolds within me. I see everything because everything is in me. I feel the orgasm climbing and climbing until I explode in his mouth, breaking against his forehead.

Slowly, my body relaxes. My voice relaxes. Everything relaxes.

He stops. Sits up. He slowly releases the valve on the cup and lets the air out. All at once, a flood of relief caresses my back. He sets the cup in the box. Moves to the next one and releases it as well. He takes the remaining two cups off me and, with every release, I feel the orgasm continuing to caress me. These are the cuddles afterward; she's still with me, bringing the offering of healing straight to the heart of the pain.

I lie there, quiet, an Alpine lake in summer. A stream of oxytocin gapes open in me, released by the cups. Tom smiles at me, kisses my cheek. He covers me with a thin blanket, turns off the light, and leaves the room.

# Inside, All My Furnaces are Ablaze

She doesn't even need to get close. I'm wet just being near her. Her boyish body, barely clothed. Those ninety-year-old eyes and Mowgli fingers that I know—all of me knows—what they know how to do to me.

She lets me simmer with anticipation. "I want to examine you under a microscope," she says. "I want to explore you with a telescope. I want to discover all the galaxies in you." She speaks, and I grow wetter.

It's been a week since we saw each other. The build-up happens between work, home, the beach. Until recently, I didn't know she existed and, here I am, draining into her. I undress before her in layers. First clothes, then stories, then secrets. The geology of the soul. I bare myself to her more and more, shedding veils of personality. Take me like this, fucked up and perfect. She takes.

She approaches. Here, it's about to come true. The moment I've waited for. It's so sweet that we linger in it another moment, close, so close, but not touching yet. Inside, all my furnaces are ablaze.

The first touch is enveloping. Interlocking. For days, I've been immersed in her—hallucinating her, writing to her, thinking about her day and night. Here it comes. Her scent arrives first, clouding my mind through my sinuses, like a bouquet of flowers entering a home on Sabbath. Then my cells sharpen to sense her skin. The muscles in her hands. Her arms. It's addictive—this is some good shit.

When she touches me, I'm at the source, before all explanations explain themselves. Reality and truths turn me upside down. Defenses crumble, closets collapse. "I will stand my armies at your service, my queen," she wrote to me, and I stood at attention. I undress and undress before her. She claims more and more parts of me.

Lavender, chocolate and strawberries surround us. In front of the huge mirror, I see her seeing me seeing her.

I see two she-wolves playing in a meadow in the mirror. Two she-wolves howling at a red moon. I see my beauty through her. Show her her beauty through me. The revolving doors in a game of duplicates, worlds colliding, meteors splashing everywhere.

When I arrived at her place this evening, there were walnuts on the table, chocolate, and a bowl of strawberries. She had walked barefoot through the kibbutz fields, picking them straight from the vine. Her ankles were stained a deep purple.

She broke off a small piece of chocolate, added a strawberry, and served it directly to my lips. Then, she slipped her finger in as well. A rave of free radicals broke out on my tongue.

"Holy moly, how many lessons I have to learn with you, she-wolf," she says. "This is what strikes me. This is what suits me."

It's her and me now. The winged Amazona that she is, and my Wendy wings lead us to fight pirates, to practice love.

My desire registers at 8.8 on the Richter scale. I need her inside me now. Need burning, need depth. I need her, the enchantress of my pussy. I need her to fuck me with her thousand hands. All the forest animals that came with her are waiting outside the door. It's just the two of us here.

"I'm clay in your hands," I tell her. "I'm all woman between your hands. Take me with you to shake the heavens." She takes.

I try to explain to Tom what happened with Noga, and what it means now—with Mowgli. I'm not even sure myself; I only know that I must go through this journey. "I'm learning," I offer, pulling an explanation from the ambiguity. "She's a mega-lesbian, and I need to understand things about my body." It seems he understands the words I'm saying, even if not their meaning for me.

Out of guilt, I encourage him to open the relationship on his end as well. He hesitates, then shortly after creates a profile on Tinder.

## Reality Beats Any High

I sprint along the sandy trail, low burrs flanking both sides. An Israeli August bequeaths to September only thistles and cracked earth. With the coronavirus, cities marked 'red,' and protesters burning at Balfour Street, I feel the earth's fire beneath my feet. Yellow running shoes, stride after stride, I pant heavily.

It's been a while since I've gone for a run, but this week everything seemed to be closing in on me. When I'm out of breath—I run. When my breathing grows labored—I run. The homeopathic principle of 'like cures like' holds true for me now too. I race my heart to calm my breath.

I feel my breasts move in rhythm with my strides. My arms pump. The pressure inside my skull throbs with each step. He, who was once mine, is now with some other woman. I feel like dying, but I'm the one who pushed him into it. Exclusivity traded for freedom—I made a deal. I freed him to free myself. Fucking hell, it's painful.

He's with some other woman so I can graze in open fields. So I can run through meadows. So I can scream at the kibbutz. He's with her because, otherwise, the guilt would choke me. Suffocation in exchange for release from suffocation. I'm no longer sure I'm such a savvy businesswoman. How many walls must my head slam against before I wrap my mind around the wild, uncompromising, sole idea that's possible for me?

Foot chases foot. Sweat drips down my forehead. A sultry Israeli night spurs my legs onward, pushing against my constricted chest. The sandy path absorbs my steps, my weight, my sorrow. Something flits by—perhaps a bat—but, as it nears, I realize it's unmistakably an owl. I halt abruptly.

She glides toward me, wings outstretched, face turned fully to the side. Hovering above, barely two meters separate us. Her eyes, direct and unflinching, lock onto mine. I'm rooted in place, mesmerized by the night owl's penetrating gaze.

Seconds pass—maybe mere fractions—yet time stands still. The owl lingers, then slightly tilts and resumes her silent flight back the way she came.

It takes me a moment to resume running. I know, I'm utterly certain, it was female. My steps falter again in the sand before finding a steady rhythm, and my heart pounds forcefully, not just from exertion. I feel oxygen rush through my windpipe to my lungs, and I discover I have an abundance, an overflow of air.

# Conference Call

I'm perched naked on her living room couch, an earbud nestled in my right ear. I'm on a conference call with Tim from London, Vanessa, my intern, and two managers from one of our subsidiaries.

We're an A-team tasked with ensuring all our products are top-notch and meet deadlines. We have a daily conference call at eight pm—this time, in my case, in full nudity.

An afternoon meeting had been cancelled, so I bee-lined to her place straight from work. I'm a crammer, getting my needs met as befits a busy manager. I squeezed in three hours with her before the call.

We're both naked, post sex and conversation, conversation and sex. I'm focused on the call but my eyes are on her. She stands in the kitchen. Naked. With that ass.

Tim explains that section 2.6.1 is missing a crucial component. Reuben will call Tony in Madrid tomorrow, who'll fill in the missing information by tomorrow evening. Vanessa updates the Excel sheet.

She looks at me. I can't concentrate when her eyes meet mine, so I lower my gaze. She turns to boil water. Now her back and ass face me, and I can stare freely. Component 4.3.3 is on schedule and being passed to the QA team for examination.

Her curls cascade from black to orange through deep brown shades, spiraling from her head. The top layers are sun-bleached from her two years in South America.

She adds lavender and honey to each cup, then pours boiling water. I'm half-listening, toggling Tim's voice—describing the updated schedule in his British accent—on and off in my mind. Ass and curls. Beneath, doe legs. Smooth honey all the way to the soles of her nomad feet.

She returns to the couch with the tea. Sits across from me. Drapes her legs over mine. I stroke them. I mute my phone and listen with my right ear. She's before me. Wild and grounded like fire in a stone circle. I caress her face, trailing along her cheek. My finger traces her lips. She bites it.

My right finger is between her teeth and she slowly, steadily increases the pressure. It hurts and her eyes bore into mine. I feel my pussy dampen and know my eyes are wide. I never knew one finger could feel such pain.

Though she's sitting here in front of me, it's as if she's rooted deep in the earth. Motionless. Deep in my eyes. Unblinking. Biting. Hard. Harder. In my ear, the team updates each component's status. I'm at the edge of pain. I cross it. I want it to end. Enough. She bites harder.

Her eyes pierce mine. So deep I think she's peering into my soul. It hurts so bad I can't take it anymore. But I can. She's with me, intense eyes locked on mine. Never leaving me. Biting steadily. God, it hurts so much. I cling to her gaze. Hang on with all my visual focus. I look at her and see a she-wolf. I want to growl and roar. To shake off the pain, but I'm frozen. Component 6.3.2 will be out of development two days late. The pain is searing. All at once, she releases her bite.

Electric currents dissipate through me. Everything I thought I was is set free, along with my finger. She lays gentle lips where she bit. Tears well in my eyes. But don't fall.

# Open Heart

He plunges his hand into the center of my chest, delving deep into my ribcage to grasp my heart. The hairs on the back of his hand are sticky with hot blood. My heart contracts and expands in his large hand, systole and diastole beating in unison.

My pussy gapes as he fucks me, his cock sliding in and out. His hand remains steady on the heart tissue, enveloping the atria and valves. The aortic valve rests between his index finger and thumb.

All the harsh words he's ever hurled at me ricochet in my head, threatening to halt the flow and output of blood, but he won't allow it. The children he created with me. The children torn from me.

With long fingers, he pumps rhythmic contractions. My life's engine in the palm of his hand.

He fucks my soul back and forth. His chest muscles glisten with sweat.

The connective tissue between my abdominal muscles stretches to near-rupture, a ventral-abdominal chasm widened by each child who grew within me, distancing me from myself.

He squeezes and releases his hand at a steady pace, performing cardiac resuscitation on me. A potent aroma of pussy and blood, iron and sweat, permeates the room.

He splits me open with his cock. My pussy is open. My belly is open. My chest is open. I'm still tight.

Dark demons perch on my lungs, spreading like tar across my bronchi. I feel I might stop breathing at any moment, but he, the bastard, presses on my heart. Unrelenting.

If I had tears, I would cry and beg him to release me.

Everything here in the bed is wet, yet somehow my tear ducts are bone dry. "You're strong," he tells me. "Remember. You've had death pass through you. You've had life pass through you." He fucks and thrusts.

He won't let go until I promise to seal my skin back together. Son of a bitch, the way he traps me with no way out.

I know the demons and curses will remain trapped under my skin even after he withdraws, even if the skin knits and scars over. I promise anyway.

# Goddess Worship

I step into her home, waiting for her to fuck all my organs. From the moment we met, I melt all walls for her. She gallops to the heart of the kingdom in my pussy. "My queen," she calls me, and my palms tremble. I stand in her living room as she looks at me. She doesn't approach. Doesn't touch. She penetrates me with the stare of a she-wolf. Opens me wide with her wild eyes and predator's teeth. It's that look that wets me to my knees. I bathe in the grace of her gaze as she slowly approaches. Slowly she inhales my scent. Slowly she growls around me. Circles me, encloses me. She does everything slowly, stretching seconds into long minutes. I continue to drip slowly.

"On your knees," she commands. I obey. She sheds her thin tank top and linen pants. She wears nothing underneath. If it were up to me, she'd walk naked in the world 24/7. There's no logical reason for a body like hers to be covered. Thank God she's only clothed around her nakedness. I sense her pussy close and my heart pounds fiercely. I offer my tongue, my mouth wet like a bitch begging for meat.

She draws nearer, finally acquiescing. She grabs my hair and I growl, extending my tongue to start licking. Clitoris. Lips. She yanks my hair, hard, and I growl between the folds of her pussy. She fucks my mouth and with every tug of my hair I receive her more intensely. My tongue laps at her, my lips French kiss her labia.

I absorb her nectar into me and I'm ready for the world to stop. Her pelvis grinds against my face. I'm consumed with longing for her, eager as a lioness. With every movement, she puts together the pieces of my disassembled puzzle. Through her heart she flows to her pussy, through her pussy she wets my heart.

Suddenly she grabs my hair and pulls me up to stand before her. I gaze deep into her eyes. We both pant. "Now come to bed," she says. I come.

## When You Come to Fuck Me

*When you come to fuck me*
*Be as gentle as a heron*
*Your touch, a flutter*
*Approach slowly*
*Until I beg*
*Even then, hold off*
*When you come to fuck me*
*Arrive like a sweet feminist*
*Pause*
*Lick, melt, wait*
*For me to get wet, for me to drip*
*And then*
*When I writhe, when I moan*
*When maybe turns to yes*
*Yes. Yes!*
*All at once*
*Impale me*
*Like a gladiator*
*Like a son of a bitch*
*Cross the sea within me*
*Like an Indian black tiger*
*Stalking an antelope*
*Fuck my shape away*
*Chain me to the bed*
*Deliver me*
*Salvation*

## When You Decide to Cross Boundaries

*When you decide to cross boundaries,*
*be ready for the cacophony that follows.*
*Be ready for scorn, be ready to be worshipped,*
*Be ready for speed—the dragons you'll ride won't pause.*
*Breathe deep; the air thins*
*Where you'll soar.*
*Be ready for multi-orgasms to tear you apart*
*and piece you back together.*
*Be ready to become elastic, to liquify, to turn mercurial.*

*When you decide to cross boundaries,*
*be ready to mother yourself,*
*For no one will forgive you, no one will show you mercy.*
*Steel yourself for criticism, for poison-tipped arrows.*
*Hold tight. This will hurt.*
*Be ready to root yourself in dust-caked earth,*
*to stand atop windswept cliffs,*
*To howl at the moon, to crack open under the sun.*

*When you decide to cross boundaries, be ready for mayhem,*
*For magic shows, for fast forward, slow motion.*
*Be ready to be scratched, opened, hurled, rattled, redeemed.*
*Prepare to anoint yourself with frankincense,*
*To rule a transparent kingdom, crowned in glory.*
*Be ready to stand alone before the righteous with their pitchforks,*
*To face the slobbering masses who will call you whore, slut, witch.*
*They won't swallow you, accept you, or let you in.*
*Be ready to be brave.*

*When you decide to cross boundaries,
be ready to run with she-wolves,
To sing with the mad under moonlight, to witness astral visions,
To be swallowed by caves, to vanish in crevices,
to taste colors with your tongue.
Be ready for the sky to open beneath you,
to fall upward into its embrace.
Prepare to breathe in copal's smoke, to glow in darkness,
To grasp fleeting lights in your hands.
Winged beasts, naked fairies,
shadows of forgotten infants will trail you.
Be ready to love them too.*

*When you decide to cross boundaries,
mandalas will entwine your fingers.
Be ready to be buried in sand, a bamboo straw your lifeline,
To sleep like an infant in the soft earth, like a crone, like a queen.
Be ready to come, screaming,
Your body too small a vessel for its burning.*

*When you decide to cross boundaries,
walk with elephants, peacocks, and horses.
Be ready to fuck God, to fuck the waves,
To fuck the air swirling between your thighs.
Prepare to open your body, consent to its tearing,
Only to discover the divine presence chose you
to guide her to herself.*

*When you decide to cross boundaries, find yourself a sister,
One who will laugh with you till your cheeks seize,
a sister who is precise in pain, soft.
A nurse, a caregiver, a sister with steel in her core,*

*Strong enough to hold all the cosmos with you.*
*Be ready for dragonflies to rain down, illuminating your nights.*
*Prepare for paper folds, for origami birds*
*To cross your shoulders on fluttering wings.*

*When you decide to cross boundaries, brace for blows to the gut,*
*To crack, to bleed, to be torn apart.*
*Be ready to drive your fist into the earth, again and again,*
*To stretch your toes forward, heels back,*
*To rise with clenched jaw,*
*Until you tower two meters ten,*
*Until wings ache where they meet your shoulder blades,*
*Until fire blazes from your eyes and there is no one left to tell you*
*That you've crossed the boundaries.*

# From the Depths of the Den

I arrive famished for her. Peeling off my dress, I'm left in black underwear. A black panther. Dark desires. I circle her, growling, purring. If a look could prey, she'd already be bleeding.

From behind, I gaze at her back dotted with beauty marks. At her ass. At her neck that smells so delicious. I keep circling. Why do you have such big eyes, Elinor? So that I can see you better. My fangs gleam. I signal with my eyes, and she walks to the bedroom. I follow, licking my upper lip in anticipation of the feast.

"On all fours," I command. She complies. I stand behind her, burying my hand in her curls, grabbing and pulling. I'm the hunter, she's my bounty—she must know it. I feel her pussy heating up, my own wetness surging. Her scent drives me wild; I want to devour her whole, but not yet.

I release her hair and clamp onto her neck from behind. My pincers lock on her. She's spread open before me, her ass and pussy begging. They're wet with anticipation's vibration. I raise my hand and smack hard. The sound is red. She moans. I smack again. She's mine now. Witch-black hair is the royal crown on my head.

I seize one of her nipples, pinching hard as she loves. I increase the pressure. Her wavelength tightens, sharpens. My fingers are firm; any harder and her nipple might tear off. So I pinch more. The nipple is strong and flexible against me. She can take the pain.

All at once, I penetrate her. Pussy and ass. The entire universe works through my fingers now. I let the intensity flow through me in a torrent. Her roars escape. She opens to the pain and terror, gives everything, takes everything. I'll tear the meat from her bones. I'll suck her marrow and leave nothing behind.

I fuck her, one hand opening worlds, the other gripping her nipple. I fuck her harder and harder. Pinch beyond the boundary of pain. I bite her neck, knowing it will leave a circular shark-tooth mark for hours.

I continue pressing and pinching, biting and fucking until she soars on a thermal column of pleasure, until her muscles relax between my teeth, until her pussy squirts on the mattress, until concepts vanish and all that remains are howls. My pains spill in a waterfall straight into her. In bones and blood I come to her, am burned to her, melted. Her dark demons crawl to me and are purified in a scream that passes through her.

She's gathered to me through hands and womb and extended legs. I embrace her, kiss her gently. Life itself has spilled between us and a new breath is born. We are empty and full of everything, close to ourselves.

"You've got that look on your face," she says, "that face that is just you."

# My Heart, Born

"Tell me about your births," she requests. Child-free by choice, she's sweet and attentive to everything about my life, my career, and my children. Always interested. At first, she wanted me to describe how Tom and I fucked, but later it made her jealous and she asked me to stop. Valid. I stopped.

"I want to know the reality of your womb," she asks so tenderly.

"I'll tell you about Lev's birth," I say. "Michaela, who was born at Ichilov hospital, was seven, and Luna, who was also born at home with Ronit, was three." (Mothers, I explain, measure time by their children's ages.)

During dinner, I start to feel back pains that feels like contractions. I ask Tom to take the girls to their grandmother. When they leave, I slip into the bathtub. I lie in the hot water, a great whale with a round belly protruding from the water's surface.

I close my eyes, feeling the warm water enveloping me, and then my father's image appears before me. My beloved father, who passed away two years ago, emerges as an infant. He, too, was a third child. Then I see my grandmother, Hannah, his mother, an extraordinary woman I knew only through stories. She was here before me in this world, in this city, Tel Aviv, and here she gave birth to the baby who would become the man who became my life's rock. Suddenly, I grasp the connection to previous generations and those yet to come, to the women who gave birth, are giving birth, and will give birth in this world. I am a conduit, passing life through me, a vessel in the kingdom of creation. I cry and laugh in the water, for I missed my father so deeply and I am overjoyed that he came to me. Now I can leave the bath. Now I can give birth.

Meanwhile, Tom returns and begins organizing the house, preparing the pool in the living room. We're both excited.

I speak to my belly, telling the baby that I trust him and I'm waiting for him. I tell him it's happening now, not to be afraid, that we're in this together.

At midnight, the contractions become more frequent, every four minutes, and I ask Tom to call Ronit. I can no longer speak on the phone; the waves wash over me. Tom calls Ronit, waking her from sleep: "Elinor is asking for you to come."

She answers: "Ole!! Ask her to wait for me to give birth." I smile.

I walk back and forth in the bedroom. When a contraction comes, I lean against the wall, both palms pressed against its cool surface. I move, move. Contractions every three minutes. Each one more painful than the last. I grunt with the contractions. My hips sway in a figure-eight, the infinite movement of the pelvis. It happens by itself. I'm there. I'm inside the movement. The contractions are unlike any pain I've ever known. When the contraction comes, I'm in terrible pain. When it's gone, I feel nothing at all. Between contractions, I breathe. Gather strength. Wait.

Tom is in the living room, speaking with Ronit on the phone who is guiding him to fill the plastic pool. This much water up to the first ring. This temperature. He says to her: "Everything is under control." I know I'm in good hands. I can't look at the bright light of the cellphone anymore so I stop timing the contractions. They are frequent and I surrender to the sensations which are stronger than me. I'm in the flow, I'm part of the birth, I'm washed over, my mind empties itself. I'm all body.

Ronit arrives at one in the morning. She comes into the

bedroom, looks at me and says: "Amazing!" If there is one word that I needed to hear—that was it.

Ronit joins me in the contractions. When she puts her hands on my back and moves with me, it hurts less. She asks if she can examine me. I can only use short syllables.

"Yes," I growl. She slides her hand to my vagina and examines me.

"Dilated to seven centimeters," she says. "Soon you're giving birth." I know it myself, he's close, this kid is galloping to us.

The pool is ready and Tom calls us to the living room. Ronit lights candles. Tom covers the lamp with a cloth. The light is soft and perfect for me. While walking to the living room, I shed my shirt and then ease into the warm water. My head rests on the rim of the pool, my arms are out of the water, and I'm on my knees, moving with the contractions which are intensifying.

I'm in pain. Pain pain pain.

I can't surf over the surface of the pain like I did with my previous homebirth. It angers me, frustrates me that I'm in so much pain. I feel the intense pain and resist it. I grunt, I sigh, I'm in constant motion. Don't stop moving.

Tom sits on the couch in front of me and offers both his hands. With every contraction he makes noises with me, holds me tight. It helps. I'm on my knees, continue to move my hips, my legs. I'm inside the pain itself. Ronit massages my back, she puts Traumeel pills in my mouth, checks the baby's pulse with a Doppler machine.

With every contraction I feel him descending lower in my body. He's progressing strongly. He's progressing quickly. I feel his strength forcing me to raise the bar, to meet him, to allow him to pass through me with all of his intensity.

With my mouth half in the water and half in the air, I make 'brrrrrr' sounds, like my girls playing in the bath—I discover that it both relieves me and makes me laugh.

"Don't push!" Ronit says. I'm not here anymore, my body does whatever it wants. What it knows. I open. Noises come out of me. I'm on all fours in the water, wiggling. My head is now pointing in a different direction. I don't know how I got here. "Do you feel like you need to push?" Ronit asks. No. But everything opens in me. My mouth, my vagina, my anus. Everything is open, passes through me, there's no me at all. Body, a tool in the water. Water water water water water mother mother mother mother mother mother.

I see Tom somewhere in front of me in the living room, feel Ronit somewhere behind me. Everything moves, everything is happening, everything is moving. I wiggle on all fours in the water, grunting, twisting. I feel sexy, beautiful, powerful.

I feel my vagina burning. I'm a tigress, I'm a tiger in the middle of the night in the jungle of Tel Aviv, cutting the air with my grunts, fucking God, riding the waves of pain and passion, water and blood. I'm dancing this child out into the air of the world, all the grandmothers helping me now to contain this wild feeling of pressure.

There is no time. It's frozen or aflame, maybe disappeared. "He's right at the opening. Here, feel him," Ronit says. I put my whole finger in my vagina and feel the tip of his head. Bald, like his sisters were born. Another contraction comes over me. I feel him pushing, progressing. I put my finger in again and this time one joint is enough, the head is close. Another contraction washes over me, and his head, hard and strong, presses at the entrance. This is it—the moment of crowning.

"Stand," Ronit says to me, "Now! Stand."

What? I think to myself, I don't understand how it's even possible to get up. I'm on all fours in the water and the head is at the opening of my pussy, but Ronit says to stand, and if there is one woman in the world who I will listen to right now—it's Ronit. Tom helps me stand up, holds me. I manage to disconnect from the warm water to stand. I don't understand why and what is happening, but I surrender. My pussy is burning, burning like it's never burned before. I'm desperate. Don't understand how the baby will come out of there. I feel his head but how? How will he come out? I'll die if he comes out. I'll be torn in two. It burns so much.

I stand in the pool. Tom and I hold each other's forearms. His palms are on my elbows. My palms grip his arms. We look at each other in the eyes. He nods at me as if to say, hold on tight. Another contraction comes. I'm in hell, I'm in the light. I scream. I'll be torn to a thousand pieces. I'll die, I'll open and then I'll die. I consent and give everything I've got. His entire body passes, burning through my legs. He's out, he's out! Slips into Ronit's hands behind me.

I'm still standing, blood flowing from me into the pool. He's crying in Ronit's arms. She's busy with something over there. I ask her if everything is okay. I held both girls immediately after they were born. She says everything is okay and holds him out to me backwards, with his back to me. I don't dare turn him around, or even move. My body has stopped.

Ronit announces the time of birth. 01:44. She asks me to get out of the pool to stop the bleeding. He continues crying. "You have to stop the bleeding now," she says again. A calm voice of reason in this dream. Tom helps me lift my leg and then my other leg slowly over the edge of the pool. I hold the baby. He's so slippery and delicate.

I sit down, resting against the side of the pool, and finally turn him around, look at his little face.

"Champion," I whisper to him, "you're such a champion." Like a lion cub, he arrived. Strong and brave and determined.

Ronit and Tom set up a comfortable mattress for me to sit on and a pillow to lean on. I move slowly to the mattress with the slippery treasure in my arms. Ronit is still talking about bleeding, but all of me is in the new child, veiled by the discovery of his eyelids, his long fingers, the shape of his lips. Ronit snaps me back to reality. "Be in the ceremony," she says, her eyes locking with mine. And I get it. Okay, stop the bleeding. Ronit changes the sheets, examines my vagina. Tom is on one side of me. Sets his head on the floor. I think he's crying.

I'm afraid to give birth to the placenta, afraid of the pain, afraid of anything passing through my vagina again and hurting me. Ronit asks me to breathe and relax. I relax and the placenta slips out.

The boy is aware of everything around him. Attentive to Ronit who goes to bring me a glass of water. Attentive to her when she goes to the other room to speak on the phone. Feels everything, sensitive. The thought crosses my mind: the name we thought of, Lev, the Hebrew word for 'heart'—yes. It fits him.

Tom cuts the umbilical cord, the third time in his life. Ronit weighs the baby with the stork scale she brought with her. 3.940 kilograms. She examines the placenta. "Big baby, big placenta," she says. The placenta is whole, and everything is fine. She hands the baby to Tom who sits with him on the bed in the bedroom, next to the radiator. "You lost a lot of blood," she says to me, "so crawl to the shower on all fours." I crawl from the living room to the shower on my hands and knees, smiling all the way. I find it funny, I'm like my girls. A trail of water and drips of blood fall on the hardwood floors, like a bride's celebratory veil behind me.

I try to rise to my feet in the shower, but my heart is beating too fast and I get dizzy. I sit under the hot stream of water, peeing, and it burns. That makes me laugh too. In the meantime, Ronit brings me clothes and fixes the sheets on the bed. When I get out of the shower she leans over me. I put my hand on her shoulder. Lift one leg and then the other. She dresses me with the gentle touch of a mother. First mesh underwear with thick pads, then pants. No shirt.

I lie in bed and she lays the baby on me, naked and wrapped in blankets. "Skin to skin," she says, "you won't be able to sleep now with the adrenaline from the birth, but later, Dad," she says to Tom, "you take the baby as well, and let Mom sleep."

The baby attaches to my breast and nurses. He's tiny and holy and perfect. He came through me like Superman. I'm so proud of him and of myself. Ronit kisses us goodbye and goes off to the next birth. Tom falls asleep next to me and I'm relaxed, the baby rising and falling on my stomach.

## All That's Missing is a Lasso

I lie naked on your bed, belly down, legs splayed. You sit astride me, upright. Your pussy dampens the back of my thigh as you grind against me, fucking me. Your fingers plunge deep inside me, matching the rhythm of your gallop. Your reins guide us, dancing us forward and onward.

Your fingers transport me to a realm beyond thought, logic, or blame. They lead me to my body, to pure spirit, to grace.

On the bedside table, there is a piece of paper with your handwriting on it. It's covered in words, but only two register: I feel. With each thrust, my body rocks on the mattress. I clutch the sheets, fists clenched. My head sways with my body. My eyes see: I feel. I feel. I feel.

You ride me, my back speaking to you. My pussy pleads, "Take me. Give me everything you've got."

We moan and growl, loud lionesses in the cricket-dotted quiet. We are lone she-wolves, united to run through meadows. We are two women in the world who found each other to practice holiness, to worship goddesses, to ascend to orange skies.

I release my muscles, letting your energy flow through me. Your fingers are like a cock, like three cocks, each igniting a different erogenous zone, sending electric currents and signals. Vitality surges here now. A carnival of senses. The universe itself courses through our veins. We don't just live in it; it lives in us.

I burn on your fingers. Sounds escape me, heard and felt, but uncontrolled. We shred the silence, adding jackal howls to the crickets' song. I'm wired to your fingers inside me. You move with determination. We breathe, we vibrate, wet. You're on one side of my pussy, I'm on the other side of yours, both of us clutching pleasure at its ends.

    I arch my back, I soar. You yell, your voice rising in volume and pitch, and I'm with you, feeling your excitement, rising too. My heart races, my breathing quickens, your juices on my thigh, my juices on your hand.

    You roar and fuck, you ascend and ascend. I'll come if you come; I'm on the edge. I hear you screaming and I melt into the lava between us. It washes over me, and I burst over you like a wild geyser. Interconnected orgasms. Woman in woman.

# Coffee

Two men stand in line for coffee, chatting—friends or colleagues of some sort.

First you order at the register, then collect your coffee, then find a table.

They finish ordering and step back to wait. I move forward, place my order, then retreat to make room for those behind me.

I position myself behind the men, next to the pastry counter, watching the barista dispatch coffee to waiting customers.

The men talk to each other. One is tall and fat, the other short and slightly less so. Both are balding, but the tall one has kept the hair on the sides of his head, growing it long.

I observe the barista's swift hands, my thoughts drifting to Michaela—did she take enough food to school today?

"Nice tattoo," I hear. I turn to see both men eyeing me. The tall one with the thinning hair has ejected these words.

"In what universe do you think your opinion interests me? What on earth makes you, a total stranger—and such a non-aesthetic, borderline disgusting creature at that—think you can comment on the tattoo I chose to get?" I don't say.

Instead, I fix him with my most piercing gaze, willing my thoughts to penetrate his skull without a word spoken.

I turn back, eyes on the barista, awaiting my coffee.

The men resume their conversation. The world slips back into its natural rhythm.

Decades-old habits aren't broken with a look, but hey, I'll keep trying.

# Bye Baby

She couldn't contain my feverish desire to conquer the world. She was small; my desire was intense and terrifying. It was okay for me—my desire and I embraced each other. Its flame was my fountain.

I drank from this mighty spring of desire, rode its waves. I barely needed food; the desire filled me. I remained thin and in constant longing.

And there were the gaps between us. I had Tom, the kids, who need what kids need, a demanding job and, when the waves came, I was at the beach, no matter what. She had me. She didn't work, intending to leave Israel once the coronavirus subsided, living on her savings. She had no children, no other relationships. She spoke often of non-hierarchical polyamory. Her arguments were eloquent; she was fluent in the language. In reality, she waited for me to come to her twice a week, whenever I could find the time.

Gaps are difficult to sustain. Like a fissure between two landmasses—sometimes it's narrow enough to jump across, sometimes the continents drift too far apart. The bridge we built dissolved and sank into the water.

I'll always be grateful for her generosity, for running together in the meadow, for the openness of her pussy (her heart? Her pussy), for how she welcomed me as a guest in her house, in her boyish body.

I returned to heeding the movement my desire dictated. My mountain-moving desire, my scream into eternity. My desire awaited the dimensions of a queen. A woman who went boom, who was wow. A woman who embodied inspiration, bravery, abundance, colors, genius, overflowing. A woman who would sweep me off my feet and then fly me to outer space. I had a ways to go before I would arrive.

Third Portal

# SHIRA, FOR A MOMENT
## 2020

# Dr. Shira

I met Shira on Tinder. She appears under a pseudonym with a blurry profile pic, writing that she's married to a man and looking for connections with women. When we transition to chatting on WhatsApp, I discover a beautiful woman, a neurologist. She's married to a man who works at a start-up company, and they have five-year-old twins.

"Discretion is important to me," she writes. "Except for my husband, nobody knows I'm with women, and it's best that nobody ever finds out."

"Sure," I answer, thinking to myself—any deeper in the closet and we could open a carpentry shop.

It's during the pandemic and there are no coffee shops or bars open. We meet at a park in the evening. She's surprisingly tall and her perfume smells wonderful. We sit on a bench next to a picnic table and get to know each other. I bring a bottle of wine, an opener, and glasses; she brings snacks. She's well-spoken and the conversation flows. She manages to stay reserved and respect her husband's privacy while telling me about their marital difficulties. She had hoped that after her studies things would be easier, and then she had hoped that after her internship things would improve. She's beginning to understand that it will never get easier.

Her husband doesn't love that she's seeing other women, but he accepts it because he has no choice. She's afraid of disturbing the waters around the ship of her marriage, so she samples passing rafts, thinking this way she'll maintain balance. It seems strange in my eyes, but hey, I'm not one to judge. Every woman tells herself whatever she needs to keep sailing. I'm rooting for her: go Shira.

"Hey! Look!" I exclaim suddenly, spotting a hedgehog a few meters away, inching across the grass. "How sweet," she murmurs. As if hearing us, the hedgehog immediately curls into a ball. We continue talking. She explains why she chose neurology specifically, and I share my experiences working at a corporation where most of the managers are men. Suddenly, I feel something pushing against my shoe, lifting my foot. I peer under the bench and discover the hedgehog, which I think might be a female, nudging my leg.

"Wow!" I say, excited. I stroke the spines, surprised by their softness and flexibility. "Look, there's another one," Shira points out, indicating another spherical form, dark and small against the green grass.

At the end of the date, she asks me to walk her to her car. We walk toward the parking lot and talk. She takes a pack of gum out of her pocket, extracts a piece for herself and offers me one as well. I go with the flow.

"Will you sit with me for a while?" she asks when we arrive at her car.

"Sure," I answer and get in.

The car's interior belies Shira's composed exterior. The backseat hosts two booster seats, while snack wrappers and plastic bottles are scattered about. She removes her gum, wrapping it in a tissue. She offers me one, and I mirror her actions.

Before I can say anything, she grabs me by the shirt and pulls me closer. We kiss, and it's passionate. She reclines her car seat and draws me to her. She takes my hand and places it on her breast, over her shirt. She devours my mouth, feverish in her desire. Then she guides my hand between her legs, over her jeans. She sighs quickly, making noises of pleasure. Everything is fast for me, surprising and dizzying.

Suddenly she stops and says that she has to go home. I give her a little kiss on the lips and get out of her car. In the parking lot, on the way to my car, I send Dana a message: "You won't believe it, the doctor is a carnivore."

"I actually can believe it," she answers, "tell me everything."

Half an hour later I get a text message from Shira: "It was fun meeting you and tasting a bit of the animal in you."

"Good night, beautiful," I answer, "it was awesome," and add a praying hands emoji.

In the following weeks I discover that Shira is not interested in conversation, in writing back and forth, in coffee. She only wants us in bed, she only wants me in the margins. I wonder what I think about that.

# Buzzing Cicadas

"You'll come and go," she says, "and, in between, we won't speak of it." I agree because I have no other choice.

I go to her to shatter into fragments.

With a delicate hand, she holds the pieces of my body's puzzle. Using a surgeon's scalpel, she extracts shrapnel from old explosions. One by one, she draws them out. Peeling scabs. Stripping away my history.

My pain doesn't faze her; she knows it intimately. Sorrow is a stretcher we lift together. A grueling field exercise on a queen size mattress.

Her gaze softens with empathy, but hardens as her limbs move. She's polite and deadly—exactly as I need her.

Her hand knows, revealing everything. Her mouth remains silent, divulging nothing.

Desire unfurls within me, like crepe paper flowers blooming. Hedgehogs circle us, their soft spines seeking refuge. She lets me crumble between her sheets. Cicadas buzz around the fountain waters she's unleashed in me.

When I leave, I seal what was opened. Dams raised, traps reset.

We're done, until she summons me again.

## Now

What's happening now
I'm tightening into myself. Becoming precise.
As always, I want everything,
As always, I receive all I desire.
Grateful for water's magic
Grateful for water's secrets.

What's happening now
An engagement ring sparkles on a hand fucking a woman
Children more beautiful than the mind can embrace
Bonfire smoke dislodges a contact lens from an eye
A bird-sister tattooed on a shoulder
We cry with laughter under a red blanket.

What's happening now
A hand weaved with veins on a forest of chest hair
I'm in a rowboat atop liquid dreams
A heart undulates, cradled in the embrace of my limbs
Everyone wants a piece of me
And I want to lay my lips on everyone.

## Chess

"You know what I love about you?" I ask her.
"You're so cool and collected, then wild in bed."
"You're wild from the start," she replies, "never collected."

Being with her is a game of chess.
One step forward, two to the side.
She runs me sideways, raises my bar.

I lift my shirt; she licks my wounds.
I open a secret door to underground worlds,
Bravely, she dons a cape and enters.

"You come to me from all the worlds," she says.
We peel off our clothes,
Two superwoman suits discarded at our feet.

She's an elegant rainbow in my sky.
Slim and secure, she rolls with me,
Dismantling decency with grunts in my ear.

Her scent lingers all day after,
We're two queens refusing to fall,
Scrambling on a board of men, kids, careers.

"It's all or nothing," she says, "It's a zero-sum game."
I can't give everything, I don't want to be left with nothing.
She fastens me to the mattress, arms strong. Mate.

# The Dynamics of Wounds

The fight between us heats up, and I need to get out of here or I'll scream. I know it, feel it bubbling up in me like spoiled food starting to simmer. I grab the car keys, wanting to leave the house and slam the door behind me. He tries to take them from my hands but can't because I'm gripping them in my fist.

He stands in front of me. His one-meter ninety frame stands between me and the entrance door. Between me and freedom. Between me and breathing.

My distress grows; everything is closing in on me.

"You aren't leaving, we're talking," he says, then launches into an explanation of how wrong I am and how right he is, how I'm not okay and he is okay. He's standing between me and the exit, and I'm not okay and he's okay, and nausea churns in the pit of my stomach as hot blood pulses at my temples.

If I could just get out of here and be alone, I could take a deep breath and calm down, I know. But he won't let me, and I feel it climbing and climbing, all this energy trapped inside, intensifying and searching for a way to scream its way out. This can't be happening, this can't be happening, I think. I'm a grown woman who can't move. How did this happen? How can this be happening?

I have to leave, I'll go crazy if I don't leave. I tell him that it's better if I leave the house now, otherwise I will begin screaming. He stands in front of me, blocking my way. "You aren't going anywhere," he tells me. "Get over yourself and talk to me now, deal with it; why do you always have to run away?"

I pounce on him so that he'll let me pass, hitting his arms.

He's strong, he towers over me by thirty centimeters and weighs thirty kilograms more than me. He's steady as a mountain and as impossible for me as a well of sorrow.

"Move," I hit him, "move out of the way." He stands firm, not moving.

I scream, "Let me go!" He looks at me as if he's been waiting for this moment, as if thinking, 'Here she is, the crazy one.'

"Move!" I shriek, kicking, swinging my arms, thrashing against him, searching for a way out. He doesn't allow it.

The more I scream, the calmer he becomes. He stands silently before me, regarding me as if he is the very embodiment of reason, and reason is him. They're allies, comrades-in-arms, jointly blocking this monster of pure emotion.

Suddenly, I'm exhausted, the stalks inside me have been mown down. I sit. He notices the change, senses my defenses have crumbled, and knows he can now likely break through. He reiterates how I'm not okay and he's okay, I'm not okay and he's okay. I say, "Fine, okay, fine."

He doesn't care that I don't believe it, that I'm only putting on a show of agreement. It's all a performance for an absent judge, one who feels more real in this moment than our relationship, more tangible than the vows we made years ago before our loved ones. This imaginary, objective judge hovers between us as he makes his case: I'm okay, she's not okay, right? Tell her. She should thank me. She ought to be grateful.

I'm tired. So tired. I confess. You're okay. I'm not okay.

He frees the exit. Makes way for me. Now that I can leave, I don't have the energy, not even to stand up. I stay on the floor, leaning against the wall.

He shows me the wounds I've left on his skin. The keys still in my hand, my nails that had tried to claw their way to freedom have left bloody trails on him.

"Look at your violence," he says to me. "I just wanted to talk. Look what you did. Look at you."

"Sorry," I say to him in a flat voice. It satisfies him, he doesn't need more for the protocol.

He turns and walks away from me. I stay sitting, leaning against the cool wall until I have the strength again to get up and continue my day.

Fourth Portal

# TAMMY GIL
# 2021

# Party Woman

Shira was too closeted, too young, too straight. She might have worked for me a few years ago, but not anymore. I was looking for someone who could handle the depths of my love and the height of my ambitions, not another closet case, not Noga Jr.

Tammy Gil was a carnival incarnate. A social activist, a well-known Tel Aviv personality, an event producer, polyamorous—a walking party. I'd heard about her over the years; she moved in circles adjacent to mine, but our paths had never crossed.

I stumbled upon her profile on Tinder. Intrigued, I swiped right. We matched.

I flirted with her, no hesitation. She replied that she wasn't really available, she was already seeing two others—her long-term partner and a relatively new one—but that I piqued her interest.

Her 'not really available' only fueled my desire. I kept casting my line, and she took the bait.

I played it cool, determined but not pushy, I was everything I knew how to be when I wanted something, or someone. We quickly migrated to WhatsApp, continuing our sweet and spicy verbal ping-pong.

"Let's meet," she wrote after about two weeks of texting fore-play. "I want to make sure you're real. I suspect you are."

"Let's find out," I replied. We settled on seven at her place.

When I let her know I was running half an hour late, she wrote: "I've already started drinking. You'll have to catch up."

From the start, she made me smile.

I arrived at her apartment brimming with excitement. I knocked. She opened the door swiftly, clad in a tiger-print shirt and a thick gold necklace. I entered, wine bottle in hand, gave her a quick peck on the cheek, and announced I was there to catch up.

We settled in her living room. She spoke and I listened, probed, delved into the phenomenon of Tammy. She was a mile-a-minute, bursting with thoughts and opinions, her voice hoarse and rapid. It was clear she was adept at presenting herself, at these encounters were meant to test the waters of potential relationships. She drank, talked, and juggled her phone, engaging with others simultaneously. And I—I was a well of quiet in her presence.

The intensity of the bulldozer that was Tammy fit me perfectly. I sat there, entertained as she plowed through the wine bottle, talking endlessly about herself.

I couldn't stop smiling. She was bouncy, frantic, so sweet it was something else. I didn't know it then, but she would be the one to help me sever the last chains in my basement.

Within the bubbling cauldron, the overflowing personality she had constructed, the verbal circus she created around herself in every moment, I recognized something that moved me deeply. She had a certain look—desperate, torn. The look of someone who had managed to escape death.

Tammy told me about her extensive social activism for women. I was impressed. She explained that every time a man murdered a woman in Israel—meaning once every two weeks—she set up a war room. "What a terrible concept," I said. "Maybe when something bad happens, we set up peace tents instead? Listening lounges? Hug halls?"

"You should know," she emphasized, "when something like that happens, you won't be able to reach me for two days. I'm not here!" I was impressed.

After three hours of her talking and me playing the audience, she moved closer to kiss me. I could tell she did this often, skilled at first dates. Without a hint of hesitation, she slowly brought her face to mine, and we kissed for a long time. One clit led to another, and we started making out. I reached my hand between her legs, over her pants, and she came, then came again, and again. "You're making me come over my clothes!" she cried in surprise.

I wonder what she calls coming, I thought to myself. It was as easy as scratching an itch.

I stroked her arms, her face, her hair. Slowly, as she leaned against me, she melted and drifted off into adorable drunk sleep on the couch.

I continued caressing her, amused by my encounter with this perfect creature. Tammy slept on me in her living room, her head on my arm. I was slightly drunk myself and too excited to fall asleep. I wanted to capture how cute we were, but my phone was buried deep in my purse. I stretched my fingers as far as I could until I reached her cellphone, which was next to us on the couch. I'd already understood that it was always, literally always, close to her.

I opened the camera app, which you can do without entering a passcode, and took a selfie of us. In the picture, I'm smiling, my eyelids half-closed, and she, the mischievous scorpion, was asleep on me.

A few minutes later, as dawn approached, I gently withdrew my arm from under her head and left for home.

I left her a message: "You're perfect," and I meant it. Not because she had no flaws, but because I found her perfect for the role. I sensed that I could pour my hopes, my falling in love, my passion, onto her. She was strong enough; she could take it.

I loved her overflowing world, her polyamory, the thousand-and-one ways she kept busy. It suited me just fine.

I lived in a whirlwind of home-laundry-dishes-cooking-Tom-kids-afterschool activities-homework-dog-office-surfing. Tammy Gil might not have had a husband or kids, but she had times dedicated to her long-term partner, other times for her new partner, extensive social justice activism, and occasional dates.

I thought it would give me the chance to enjoy her and our limited time together, without swallowing my time whole.

I was wrong, but I didn't know it yet.

When I woke up to the kids in the morning, after just two hours of sleep and with a ringing hangover, I suddenly remembered the picture I'd taken of us. I immediately wrote her: "I took a picture of us with your phone. It might seem creepy, so be forewarned when you open your gallery." A few minutes later, she sent me back a row of rolling-on-the-floor laughing emojis.

# Loopy-Doopy Love-Struck

"You were tailor-made to my specifications," she writes, "and so is that tongue of yours."

Every free moment I have, whether it's an hour or an entire night, I go to her. Her flexible work allows her to meet any time of day. I steal time from everywhere I can, first from the office, then from the kids.

She lives as though she'll die tomorrow. I live as though I just started living today. We're two love-struck dopes, forty-something teenagers meeting to dismantle the skies.

One afternoon I write from the office that I have some free time and, if I hurry, we can have an hour together. "Come to me immediately," she says. I do, and she opens the door with that penetrating-penetrated look of hers. We kiss and go straight to the bed, as if there isn't even a hallway.

She ignites under my touch and rewires Tel Aviv's electricity. I desire her intensely, with greedy urgency.

My tongue engineers pathways around her clit. Her breathing deepens into me; I understand her through her inhales and exhales. She's a panther on a tree, a tiger-person, and I'm pathologically lustful for her.

In flashes, I see in her eyes a hint of the sad little girl she was, echoing the little girl I once was. This is what captures my heart, moves mountain ranges in me.

"All I want is for you to come back here to fuck me immediately," she writes. "Did you take in what unfolded here today?"

"I took it in very much, yes."

"Where else do you want to reach when you enter me like that?"

"I want to reach all the places," I answer. "That's exactly it."

She goes from party to party, from production to event. She has extensive social circles, three lovers, and she's never alone. Despite the bounty of people in her life, she always knows exactly what's going on in mine—with my children, with Tom. She asks, shows interest, remembers everything I tell her. She passes evenings of tequila and cocaine like others pass evenings with an omelette and salad. Compared to her, I'm goody-two-shoes girl-scout good-girl vibes. I wake up when she goes to sleep. I prepare sandwiches for school while she's emptying ashtrays and clearing empty alcohol bottles from her living room.

When she calls, I show up. I don't know how or want to tell her no. After the beach, I pick her up; she lies down in the passenger seat underneath my surfboard. With one hand on the steering wheel and the other between her legs, I make her come while I'm driving.

When her plans change and she has free time in the evening, she calls and I come. I don't know which I want more—to see her, or to get out of the house. Tom's big body takes up so much space, I need air. She has plenty of air for me.

I sacrifice hours of sleep to be with her. I sleep two or three hours, leave her in bed in the morning and quietly slip out to the office, driving in a daze. Escalation is the new normal. I function on the fuel of falling in love and longing for more. Who needs sleep and food when you have Tammy Gil?

## Brink of an Abyss

With you, there's no middle ground—always on the brink
of an abyss.
I soar on your engine to worlds without guarantees,
As logical as perching on sea cliffs, wine bottle in hand,
Like gazing into your searing, gaping eyes.

We walk hand in hand as buildings blaze around us,
Fighter jets roar above, tectonic plates shift,
Yet somehow the ground steadies beneath my feet.
There's only the next step and the path forward with mad eyes.

You say, "Nothing is under control, move on,"
And play music to sweeten the pain.
The scenery changes but it's all filled with you.
Forty years on the horizon, each moment singular,
all could end in an instant.
Nothing ever truly ends.
We weave a path to contain some fragment of the uncontainable,
Like owls exploring what kind of sanctuary we might become.
You were right, it takes courage to fall in love with you.

"I'm lucky," you say.
"It's not luck, it's brains," I routinely answer.
We slice the air with ninja strikes,
Tearing down walls, floors, and glass ceilings,
Snowboarding on patriarchy's ass.

And with all the storm that you and I are,
Together we have the quietest quiet.
You're the softest caress, the gentlest snuggle.

*We have a togetherness that creates a vast space,
it can be the size of nothing,
Between your eyes and mine,
And it's the size of cities, corporations,
swarms of people in streets.*

*The universe between us happens everywhere:
Before the Annunciation Church, under the surfboard,
In a down comforter in a desert storm, in the passenger seat.
It's love in sea, air, and land.*

*As if we don't fly high enough already,
We've signed up in advance to kite-surf the Greek sea.
We're the jackpot of soft and sexy,
A red carpet unfurls itself before us.*

*What more does one need, what?
To agree more. To surrender more.*

## You Can Do Anything

"You can do anything," my dad used to tell me in my childhood. It was the most empowering sentence, one that placed branches for me to climb to the sky.

"You can do anything," when I excelled at school and was accepted to university. "You can do anything," when I finished my degrees with highest honors and went up on stage to receive my accolades from the rector. "You can do anything," when I got a prestigious job. "You can do anything," when I started earning a high salary. "You can do anything," when all around me were only men in tailored pants and button-down shirts, men in comfortable shoes, men behind wide desks, men in beautiful offices.

There were very few women around me in key positions. There were many women in secretarial roles.

The women didn't wear comfortable clothing or shoes. Regardless of their body type, they squeezed themselves into too-tight clothes and wore high heels that distorted the shape of their feet.

High heels made us walk slower than the men. It's harder for a woman to run in heels, or to walk quickly across a parking lot when she's alone in the dark and a strange man approaches. She's more vulnerable and has to pay attention to how she places her weight as she steps forward, or she'll topple over. When you're dedicating attention to something as basic as walking, your natural flow of thoughts is disrupted. A man walks forward and talks, thinks; men walked to the dining room in groups, to the conference rooms. The women did too, but were forced into a much more complicated division of mental resources.

When you're busy sucking in your stomach, policing your thighs, smiling—I haven't even mentioned smiling yet—you're less focused on big ideas about bids, about renewable energy, about budgets.

And yet. "You can do anything." So I did.

When I gave birth to Michaela, my oldest, I was working in headhunting. I located people for key positions abroad, for CEO and VP roles in huge companies. When I say people, I mean men. It wasn't stated policy, this was just the data. Over 90% of the people in key positions were men. 100% of the qualified candidates I found, who had the right training and education, were men.

When I had Michaela, Tom took vacation days and stayed home with me for a week. We slept a lot, we laughed a ton. I was nursing, so I got up every three hours at night. After a week, he got up in the morning, showered, shaved, and put on his nice, tailored pants and button-down shirt. I remember the color. It was white with tiny blue dots. He put on a brown leather belt, sprayed himself with aftershave. Michaela was on my shoulder, half asleep as newborns are, still fetus-like. He gave me a kiss. He gave her a kiss, said goodbye, and left the apartment.

I stared at the door as it closed behind him, listening to his footsteps descending the stairs. I wore a huge t-shirt of his that functioned as a kind of dress on me. I still had a post-birth belly; I looked about seven months pregnant. My breasts were a size I didn't recognize, something between a cow and a human, and they dripped with milk. There were spit-up stains on my shirt-dress and the house was quiet. It was an eerie silence, one I didn't know how not to scream into, but I couldn't wake the baby, so I fell silent in the face of this quiet.

My email inbox suddenly stopped showing any activity. After all, I was on maternity leave, all my projects had been redirected to my replacements. The girl was in my arms because she cried every time I put her down. She weighed a few kilograms, and my back didn't hurt yet from picking her up, like it would later, when she'd grow and still want 'up.'

"You can do anything," my father told me, who had never given birth and had never stayed at home while life moved on.

I did everything. I advanced by sheer force of will, clawing my way forward with my fingernails. When Michaela was four months old, I reclaimed one of my projects, working on it from home without pay, just to maintain my grip on it, to prevent anyone else from snatching it away. In hindsight, it was a success—a year later, I received a bonus because of that project. But I repeat: I worked on it without compensation, solely to keep my hold on it.

When Michaela was seven months old, I hired a nanny and returned to the office. I worked until three-thirty, then battled traffic to relieve the nanny. I was a super-mom because I could do anything. "Playground, organic fruits and vegetables—I'd put her to sleep in the evenings and then go back to working until midnight, trying to catch up with what my colleagues, the men, had done at the office in the afternoon.

Tom would return from the office in the evening. Best-case scenario, he'd give the baby her bath while I prepared dinner. Worst-case (for me), he'd linger at work and arrive after she had already fallen asleep.

"Wow, I'm beat," he'd say. "What a day. So busy." He'd pour himself a whiskey and settle in front of the television as I opened my laptop.

I was determined not to let motherhood derail my career. "You can do anything," my father told me. But at what cost, Dad?

Within two years, Tom received a promotion and was managing a small team of analysts at his investment firm. I still had the same job. My promotion was simply not regressing. I ran at full throttle, just to stay in place.

Over the years, I did make progress but, with each birth, I fell behind again, taking years to climb back to where I'd left off. I swam with all my might against the tides.

The men developed a camaraderie amongst themselves. They were members of the same club, brothers in arms, fans of the same team. They wove their webs together, while I remained isolated. They took care of each other when positions became vacant, tipping off their army buddies or friends from previous jobs. "Dude," they called each other at the office, "bro," "my man."

Bros before hoes is a well-known rule; I'm not revealing anything new here.

The cliché that a woman has to be smarter, stronger, and more talented to be in a position parallel to a man turned out to be, like so many clichés, true.

Most men I encountered were mediocre at best. Their secret ingredient was a woman at home who took care of the kids and allowed them to move forward. I wondered how far I could go if I had a woman at home who would pick the kids up from school and care for them with the same attention these men paid to their egos. Like a Mary Poppins, but one who doesn't get paid, and who also cleans, cooks, washes, and folds the laundry.

The men seized every opportunity to glorify their achievements. The penis size syndrome didn't spare even the most educated among them. They compared ideas ("mine is better"), they compared their connections (obsessive name-dropping), they teased each other in front of the boss to stand out. I'd expect grown men to be different from high school teenagers, but no. Their bodies had developed, they were balding, their bellies had grown, but their social behavior remained unchanged from their youth.

The most brilliant women I encountered in the field of engineering projects accomplished much and spoke little. They were few in number; in a company of 10,000 employees, we were 11% women, most serving as secretaries to the oh-so-important men. I could count the women in senior positions on one hand and still have fingers to spare.

"You can do anything," my father, the wisest of men, told me in my childhood. It burned when I discovered how far that was from the truth.

## Desert Storm

*Consent has layers, it turns out.*
*She, a frenzied butterfly; I, an extravagant dragonfly—*
*We launch our desert storm operation.*
*Cocooned in a down blanket, lightning and thunder outside,*
*Love and sparks of light pour from our mouths and eyes,*
*We babble sweetness on overdrive, swim in skin for hours.*

*She's a woman unlike any other,*
*Piercing my gaze, staining every fiber and sinew with her hue.*
*She penetrates layers, mama, oh mama,*
*oh grandmama! This is truly a witch's den*
*Where horses and motorcycles mingle, flesh and heart,*
*Fire and hot water on skin, trust from other realms.*

*"Your ass is a universe," my sweet-spicy love declares.*
*How is it that, between us, each spark is both*
*fleeting and eternal?*
*With her, it's always present progressive,*
*I climax in her mouth and weep in her arms,*
*Miniature demons escape my eyes in droplets*
*For there's a limit to what the body can contain.*

# Questionably Sane

"You're Super Mario on acid, all my receptors are open to you," I write to her.

"My pussy is on fire from you," she replies.

"Like an intensifying hot spring, this thing between us," I write.

"Wow, what are we going to do?" she asks.

"The only thing we can," I answer.

I know her with closed eyes and open hands. She is magnificent defiance of logic, a flame in the core of my belly. Her scent, gentle and silent, enters me, climbing from my nostrils to disperse in my brain like a mist of such soft madness. I roam over her face and body, listening to the nerves at the tips of my fingers. She ambushes me from every corner. She bends me so far, and reveals to me that I am more flexible than I thought.

She comes simply. I get on her mouth and make myself come. I push so hard that she cuts her lips with her teeth from the rubbing.

"You're an outer-space supercharger," she calls me when I want to check how many volts she can take. She is challenging and she doesn't give in and I know that she knows the way to insist on freedom.

I wonder if she's bored of sex, because she fucks like someone who has done it all and has nothing left to discover. She goes through the motions, does everything right, but is predictable. It goes against her image and loud personality. "Is the sex with me too vanilla for you?" she asks. I'm not bothered because I'm excited enough just from being with her, and I know that my sexuality will develop along other lines than with her (yay polyamory). The banal sex doesn't contradict my intense desire to be close to her, so I summarize the second part of my answer and simply answer, "No."

Words have that magic power: even when they are true, they are deceptive.

"She's make-believe," Dana tells me. "She's all air."

Dana is my genius friend, but I'm falling in love with Tammy Gil, a woman who is a bungee-jump. She has a penetrating and naked stare, she has the gut of a pirate when it comes to tequila. Against all this, there is her, quiet in my arms, in all of me wrapped around her. "As soon as I throw myself at you, everything works out," she says. The woman who doesn't know how to be quiet manages to relax and fall asleep in my arms. There, in the eye of the tornado, over the ribs, there is an island of sand and sun and we both glitter on it. I'm proud to give her what no one else can. I'm still not thinking about the price.

"Tigress..." Tammy writes to me in the middle of a workday at Build and Renew. "Might have the option of meeting today. Not sure how, but everything bends to your will."

"No, you, no words," I answer her, "Do you enjoy torturing women trapped in the office?"

"In your case—tigresses trapped in a cage."

"It's self-defense," I write her. "We can't roam free."

"I've noticed."

"Bleeding bodies everywhere, not nice."

"The tigress who did me," she writes, "and I survived to tell the tale."

I come to her again and again and again. I lie on top of her, face to face. I dampen her pants, leaving white rivulets on her. My clitoris hardens in her hand as she whispers in my ear, "You have no idea how much wider your wings will still unfurl." She spins discs of pleasure for me, orchestrating a festival in the heart of my pussy.

How crazy am I to agree to come on her neck? To come on her mouth in Nazareth before the Church of the Annunciation, in front of the tree in her bedroom window? To down a shot of tequila with her after first shedding all our clothes? My mind reels at the radical notion of releasing all my fears with her.

On days we're apart, I'm with the kids, at home, at the office, at the beach. In between, we text obsessively. I'm not truly present anywhere—I'm on my phone, engrossed with Tammy and, when I'm not, I'm thinking of her. I perform the actions, already skilled at functioning in all arenas of my life, but I'm aware I'm in a frenzy. If, for a moment, I think everything's fine and I'm okay, Dana reminds me—it's not, and I'm not.

## The Transparent Heart

*"Speak words to me," she says,*
*While he, he asks for kisses,*
*To love him entirely through his cock,*
*All condensed to a bulging emotion.*

*"Tell me everything," she asks,*
*I do not know how to serve her the right words*
*In perfect cadence,*
*But I do know how to melt cocoa butter in a bain-marie,*
*To grind coffee beans, a touch of maple,*
*Mix, freeze, and slice into angular shards*
*This erupting emotion of mine.*
*She savors it.*

*English lessons. A caress. An embrace. A Lego police helicopter,*
*Glittering fractals on the living room floor.*
*I ask, though I know the answer,*
*I have no choice but to go and return.*
*Soft hair slips between my fingers,*
*Everything intertwines with everything.*

# Life, Death, Words, Deeds

It's late evening when Tammy receives a call. She places her hand over the phone and says to me quietly, "It's important, I need to answer." She puts it on speaker—a conference call with four women. They're discussing another woman who fled her home this evening, escaping her violent husband. She left with two children, only the clothes on their backs, and she doesn't know what to do. She reached out to someone who contacted Tammy and two others, and now they're talking.

The call lasts an hour. Tammy explains about hidden shelters at secret addresses so the violent men can't find them. She outlines the law, social services, detailing the options available to the woman.

"What you do is so important," I tell her when the call ends. "I know I've saved at least two women from death," she replies, "and dozens more from a horrifying fate." I'm moved by her.

"How are you?" I text Tammy midday. I'm at the office, decoding bid committee protocols, parts of them redacted in precisely the most interesting places.

"Honestly?" Tammy replies.

"Always," I answer.

"I'm organizing a funeral," she writes. She has a close friend, Maya (Tammy being Tammy, they're exes who still sleep together occasionally). "Maya's sister killed herself."

Tammy gives me some background on the sister, on the death. We're supposed to meet tonight but, given the sad event,

I tell her she can feel free to cancel if it doesn't feel right for us to meet at a time like this.

"No way," she answers, "I really want to see you."

"So do I," I reply, "You can unwind under my touch, it'll be good, we'll transform the shit."

In the afternoon, Tammy and her friends attend Maya's sister's funeral. I'm with the kids. Tom and I are in sync—tonight I won't sleep at home, tomorrow night he won't. This new arrangement works well for us; we've found a practical symmetry.

I think about Tammy. I hope she's doing okay, as much as possible under the circumstances. At some point, I get a message from her: "It was heavy and sad, just left, come to me at seven."

I arrive to find a good portion of a tequila bottle already inside her. She says, "Come to bed, tonight we drink to her memory." Her hoarse voice is now thick with alcohol. I feel her pain cutting from within. I've never seen her like this. She speaks slowly, her gaze not really here.

We fuck in the sadness, it's mostly a caressing-fuck. Every so often she reaches for the bottle she's placed on the nightstand and drinks straight from it. She offers it to me, but I decline, and she slurs: "You're not keeping up," stretching the words out slowly. Forming a complete sentence is challenging for her.

I understand the relationship between pain and tequila, and she's a big girl, but still, this image burns itself into my memory: an articulate, sharp-tongued woman, slowly extracting words from her throat and collapsing into sleep.

The next day, Tammy tells me she hit on someone at the funeral. The someone, Natalie, is a childhood friend of the deceased, may her memory be a blessing. She's married to a man and has three children. Natalie has never been with a woman, and she was very excited when Tammy made a move on her.

# The Cat's Out of the War Room

Two weeks after Maya's sister's funeral, another woman was murdered in Israel. Or perhaps it's time to be more precise: another man murdered his wife. After all, let's be clear, the woman didn't murder herself.

On this day, Amir Raz, a police officer, fought with his 35-year-old wife, Diana Dedbayev. He bound three of their children with rope, then placed the fourth, a baby, in a highchair. Diana screamed at their eldest daughter, nine years old, to run and call the neighbor. The girl managed to wriggle free from her bonds and scrambled for the stairs but Amir Raz, the police officer, grabbed her and shoved her down, leaving her badly bruised. He turned to Diana and plunged a kitchen knife into her thigh, twice. As Diana struggled to wrench the knife away, he drew his gun from its holster and, before their children's eyes, shot her in the head. Afterward, he, the police officer, yelled to the children: "Yay! Now there's no mom."

The next day, Tammy and Natalie went on a date.

I can't complain about Tammy; I'm no social activist myself, never have been.

Tammy has devoted much of her life to supporting abused women, or rather, women whom men abuse. She's been active in backing women's shelters, advocating for women's rights, organizing women's protests.

My activism took a different form: being a woman in a position of professional power. Being a woman in a man's world because, if I weren't there—only they would occupy those boardrooms, those spaces where decisions are made.

The most radical thing both Tammy Gil and I did for women, each in our own way, was to love them.

Supposedly-straight Natalie discovered she was intensely drawn to Tammy, that is, to women, that is, to Tammy. It seems their encounter shook her world and then her freaked-out husband. Tammy was no stranger to turning straight women lesbian; Natalie wasn't her first and certainly wouldn't be her last. Mazel tov, another baby dyke was born.

I can't complain, yet, when I learned that Tammy was spending the night with Natalie on the same day the news broke about Amir Raz, the police officer, shooting his wife Diana Dedbayev, I felt sick to my stomach.

Suddenly, I understood something about her. She moves through the world connected to women, drugs, and parties like a defibrillator. Without electric pulses to her heart, I'm not sure she can feel anything.

This led me to understand something about myself. In reality, it was I who was fighting against death through her. My bourgeois life, my corporate career, the confinement of my abstract soul in an institutional box—all of these threatened to kill me. I was crying out for freedom. She was perfect for me, she fit me perfectly. Until she didn't.

# This Chasm

I'm dismantling seventeen years of marriage.

He's shattered. Gaunt. He's grown stubble. "This is the closest I've come to death," he tells me, "I don't want to live."

He sprawls on the couch for hours. The kids are around him, playing. Sometimes he responds. Mostly, he lies with eyes closed. "Dad takes a lot of naps," they inform me.

It's been six days since I told him we're separating. That was on February 27th. Now it's early March, and I'm calculating when he might realistically move out. April, maybe?

"Give me one more chance. For the kids," he begs. He's signed up for therapy, joined a men's group. He's willing to sleep in the office, let me fuck other men, anything. He doesn't understand. I'm not there anymore.

"When I'm lying on the couch with my eyes shut," he tells me, "I'm not sleeping. I'm replaying everything. I'm beating myself up for how I was. Thinking about what I could have done differently."

"That's the tragedy," I tell him. "I waited years for that to happen. By the time you woke up, it no longer mattered."

I sign up for a kitesurfing lesson on the beach in Bat Yam. He asks to join with the kids, says they'll play on the beach during my lesson. I agree.

The instructor greets me with a smile and tanned, muscled arms. I smile through his poetic explanations, encouraging him to put on more of a show. He reveals more and more information this way. I'll only absorb about ten percent, obviously, but

I'm still aiming for the maximum. I know Tom and the kids are somewhere nearby, but only the lesson holds my interest.

The instructor straps me into the harness, hands me the bar, and stands behind me, gripping the trapeze above my waist. I wonder if it's appropriate, but I feel safe, comfortable. The situation is making me wet, and so is he, a little.

With my hands, first guided by his and then alone, I send the kite soaring skyward. The canopy rises and rises until suddenly my feet lose contact with the sand. It takes a moment to register that I'm actually airborne. After a few seconds, hovering about thirty centimeters off the ground, I feel a tug from behind and abruptly stop. The instructor pulls me back down. Now I understand his proximity is practical. It makes me surrender even more. What should be a ninety-minute lesson stretches to three hours.

Tom's sorrow hangs in the air along the entire shore. I can sense him, but I'm more attuned to the kite unfurling above me, my feet in the sand, my body lifting and falling, my arms, stomach, and knees rallying to the effort. I see beige sand, blue water, and the yellow-orange of the kite canopy. I jerk my arm too hard and the kite crashes onto the sand. "Slowly," he whispers behind me, as if we're in an archery lesson from a Disney movie with a porn twist. We gently coax the kite back into the sky.

The children are losing patience. It's been two and a half hours, it's hot, and they're tired. They approach us but don't complain. They listen to the explanations. The instructor, pleased with his expanded audience, adopts an even more cartoonish voice, and I continue to absorb every detail. At the end of the lesson, we exchange phone numbers, and he tells me to feel free to ask him anything. I try to be proper on the way to the car with the kids and with Tom, who brings a weary heaviness, but I can't wipe the smile off my face.

We climb into the car; Tom taking the driver's seat. For six days now, his breathing has been slow and labored. He eases out of the parking lot and merges sluggishly into traffic. An apartment in Bat Yam on the beach, I muse, making a mental note to look into rental prices.

"McDonald's?" the kids plead.

Our eyes meet for a piercing second before I look away.

"Yeah, McDonald's is fine," I answer.

# Bonsai Love

We weren't supposed to meet today, but she sends me a message: "Tigress, guess what? I'm free tonight."

"Tammy!! When exactly am I supposed to catch up on the 2,000 hours of sleep I've missed?"

She sends the monkey-covering-its-mouth emoji. Oopsy, she's caught me again.

I'm so exhausted, my life is like running a marathon made of sprints. Home-office-kids-Tammy-beach, rinse and repeat.

"You should come with a warning label for dangerous drugs," I write back, already knowing I'll go to her like a puppet. Sleep is for the weak.

"You're not normal," I hear Dana's voice in my head. Normal is also for the weak, I answer the voice.

She's a magnet, activating me in a way that's utterly complete, and I'm trapped in my craving. At night, I beg her to let me sleep. "I'm a mother of three, you have to understand," I tell her, "I'm missing ten years of sleep." She laughs and claims to understand, but she keeps waking me up. In the middle of the night, I find her mouth on my pussy. She gets my time the only way she knows will work.

Sleep deprivation is a well-known torture device; every Shin Bet agent and young mother knows this. Functioning for long periods at the level demanded of me requires a healthy lifestyle. Sleep, good food. The relationship with her is draining all my strength.

She listens, nods, but still wakes me up every night we spend together.

I'm drained. From party to event, drug to pick-me-up. The never-ending carnival meets my limits. She isn't healthy for me and I know it. I still stay, but I know the end is near.

I'm looking to put down roots and she's all over the place. I want to plant a forest; she offers me a Bonsai wrapped in crinkly cellophane.

I still hold the belief that this encounter with her, as she is, is making me a bigger person.

"She's sick," Dana says decisively, "and her crown is made of plastic."

"It's the heart of the child she once was that moves me to tears. It's her pain that she allows me to see." I try to explain to Dana, even though I know there's no explanation that will convince her. Within this broken child, in this woman who's been cut apart and reassembled, there are torches of intense vitality.

"Thank you for letting me enter you," I write to Tammy.

"It's because I'm not an idiot," she answers. "Anyone would want you to enter her, caress her, make her come, put her to sleep, leave and then tell her she's perfect. And want her to be polyamorous. And be an Amazon, a warrior, surfer, with an ass that's a universe."

She had a point.

Even though she's good to me, she isn't good for me.

"You know what you have to do," Dana says, "so just do it already." My tough friend undoubtedly knows how to cut off relationships.

"I'm addicted," I tell her.

"That's exactly why you have to stop."

Fifth Portal

# ESTHER LIONHEART
# 2021

# Thank You for Coming

As miracles unfold, so too did this encounter seem coincidental, yet in hindsight, it reveals itself as brilliantly engineered. It could not have been otherwise, claimed Spinoza, who understood a thing or two about the laws of the universe.

It was a warm Saturday night at the end of May. Tammy and I arrived at Ariella House—the bar, not the library—to celebrate the wedding of two of her friends, a producer and a scriptwriter. After many years together, they had decided to celebrate in white dresses at their favorite bar. Local mini-celebrities and an assortment of people in fancy attire showed up to strut their stuff and amplify their dopamine levels, while I came as Tammy Gil's 'plus one.'

Like most social events Tammy took me to, the guest of honor was cocaine. In my younger days, I'd had my share of nights of rolled-up bills and glittering promises in bathroom stalls. Out of all the mind-altering substances, some of which are still friends to this day, I never liked this liar.

Tammy's friends and she went in twos and threes to the bathroom and came back boisterous and opinionated. They tossed around imaginary script ideas and wordplay, their hyper-copywriter-ish conversation washing over me like a grotesque audiovisual spectacle. I watched them, quiet. I had already learned that there are bottomless pits, and there are experiences that can be swallowed whole.

The bar was packed to capacity. We sat outside on metal chairs around circular tables. Above us surged a rush of people. People sat in every possible chair, crowded around the bar, standing, dancing, huddled around the tables outside, on the sidewalk. The scent of perfumes, cigarettes, and alcohol fumes hovered in a cloud around us.

Tammy disappeared to the bathroom once more with another group of friends, and I was left without her at a table full of women laughing too loudly, with irony that was too sharp, about topics that were too hollow.

I was exchanging pleasantries with a couple of women sitting across the table when suddenly I saw her—Esther Lionheart—approaching.

My pulse quickened; I knew her art, her public persona. For over twenty years, her image had loomed large in my life, an icon of talent and freedom. I was still in high school when she blazed onto the art scene like a meteor. They spoke endlessly of her artistic genius, the magic she conjured with oil paints, her delicate balance between psychedelic and organic, cyborg and meditative.

At the peak of her success, she had relocated to New York and was occasionally seen walking around Tel Aviv.

Just a month ago, I'd spotted her at this very bar, perched on a high stool outside, chatting with a friend who had short bangs. I had wanted to approach but lacked the courage.

Esther Lionheart advanced in what felt like slow-motion. She had short hair and was wearing a blue tank top, her shoulders leading her motion forward. I expected her to pass by me—I didn't dare think otherwise—but she stopped next to me and then sat down in the only empty chair, next to me. She stared at me with eyes unlike any I'd seen before, luminous with the wonder reserved for youth newly awakened to the world.

She leaned her head close to mine and said, "Thank you for waiting for me."

I smiled at her, a bit confused, but thrilled.

"Thank you for coming," I replied. "Yes, I was waiting for you."

"I've been waiting longer," she said with a smile, extending her hand.

"It's nice to meet you, I'm Esther."

"I know who you are," I responded. "I admire your work."

"What a pleasure for me," she said as our handshake lingered, neither of us letting go.

"I'm Elinor," I said.

Her eyes locked onto mine, and the world faded away.

# Air Dancing Between the Clouds

My body was turned towards Esther, who sat to my left. After a few minutes, when Tammy returned from the bathroom and sat to my right, my back was slightly turned to her. I remember wondering if it was appropriate to arrive at the bar with one woman only to melt into another. I remember answering myself: Tammy hits on women left and right, after all. We're polyamorous. Everything is allowed, precisely because it's out in the open, not hidden.

The truth is, I simply had no choice. Esther's gravitational pull captivated me, pierced through me. Nothing else mattered. I don't remember what happened with the couple sitting across from us at the table. I don't recall when they got up and left, or if we even said goodbye. But I do remember every word Esther Lionheart said to me.

Ten minutes into our conversation, her eyes deep in mine, she told me we had met in a previous lifetime. She put her hand over her heart and said, "I'm excited because it's clear to me that I came here to meet you." Her eyes, wide open and sparkling—I had never seen anything so hypnotizing in my life.

For the next four hours we didn't stop talking. I focused only on Esther; everyone around me faded into a pale background.

She told me everything that mattered.

How she had been born, how her mother had insisted, despite the doctors who recommended an abortion. How she had grown up at the Sea of Galilee, and then on a kibbutz just north of it. She would ride her horse bareback, without a bridle, just a rope, clutching its mane as she galloped barefoot through the Jordan Valley.

She described taking her horses to swim in the lake, how they would enter the water with her.

She told me about windsurfing in the Sea of Galilee, the only girl then among all the boys. She demonstrated what it feels like when your body is parallel to the water. She leaned back and gripped an imaginary bar, and I could see her on the surfboard, one with the wind. I saw how strong she was, how muscular, focused. I knew that was what she wanted me to see.

She told me that she had bought a church in upstate New York to paint on its interior walls. Her breath paintings, her soul paintings, were quite renowned, and I was familiar with them. She breathes with the paint at the rhythm of her heartbeat, leaving traces on the canvas. The air inhales and exhales through her, signs of her vitality left on the canvas, on the wall, on the soul of the observer.

She told me about her ex-girlfriend in New York, a Korean-American chef. I told her that I had three children but didn't show her pictures of them. I didn't want to torture her, to be one of those annoying moms who shove their phones in people's faces and force them to look at their squirts of DNA. I smiled, I was enchanted; she looked and sounded like she was from a different planet.

She told me how she had started painting at age six and had never stopped since. She told me about the boat she lived on in the Jaffa port, how she had ordered special navy-blue sheets with gold embroidery to match the bow of the ship.

She told me about her father, a trumpet player, and about her mother, a diamantaire whose eyes sparkled when she looked at gemstones through a loupe.

She told me everything that mattered, and I swallowed every

word. I drank in her lips moving in her face with my eyes. She wasn't like anything I had ever known and, at the same time, everything about her spoke to me deeply.

There, at the crowded bar, surrounded by the commotion of the noisy wedding, I was already hers. I knew, she had already colored everything in me.

## You Saw My Wildness

You were meeting friends earlier. When everyone went their separate ways, you almost went home but, at the last minute, you decided to check out the bar. Curiosity pulled you—you wanted to see what was brewing. You pedaled your bike, arrived, and saw the bustling crowd. You stopped, locked up your bike, glanced again at the round tables on the sidewalk, and then your eyes found me.

You understood everything in that moment, you told me later. You knew.

On the short walk from your bike to my table, a mere ten steps, you made a silent vow: "I'll tell her everything, I'll give all of me. If she wants me, she'll want me as I am."

Amidst the throng, bodies pressed shoulder to shoulder, between packed tables and busy pathways, there was one available seat. Next to me. "It was waiting for me," you'd tell me later.

You told me you could see my wildness. "It wasn't just your beauty or your appearance," you explained afterward, "It was your essence—I could see your primal spirit."

You sat down and, without thinking, said: "Thank you for waiting for me."

You asked if I was here with someone. Yes, with Tammy Gil, I answered, a well-known polyamorist. "Are you two in an open relationship?" you asked. "Wide open!" I replied, emphasizing the 'wide.'

You said you were glad I was polyamorous because it allowed

us to get to know each other; but, you said, "I really, really am not." You too made sure to emphasize what was important.

You told me you believe there's one soul in the world destined to be your love. You hadn't met her yet, but you had an inner knowing that one day you would.

"You don't search for love," you told me, "You find it. When you're ripe and ready, she arrives." You said we knew each other from a previous life, that you could feel it. Your eyes burned as you spoke, your hands in motion.

You told me how the doctors had told your mother to abort you, but she refused to believe them. She lay in bed for long months, protecting you, and then gave birth to you in a quick and easy delivery. You described how she would later walk with you in the pram, going from doctor to doctor, showing them the beautiful baby you were. "This is the one you told me to abort!" she admonished them.

You told me about working in the kibbutz stables as a teenager, how you would help birth the mares—they would let only you get close to them. You drank handfuls of their fresh milk. You slept with the newborn foals so they would get used to your scent, and then, when they grew, you would tame them.

You brought your head close to mine there in the crowded bar, and whispered in my ear how much you love to eat pussy. You spoke to me in a language I understood. "When I love a woman, I love myself," you said, and the hairs on my arms stood up.

You came to me in a way that no one, ever, had before. You came straight to my soul and you brought all of you. Without hesitation, you entered and built a harbor inside me.

# Whiskey and Figs

Tammy Gil's mind unraveled a bit during those days. I was utterly consumed by Esther. We texted while I was at work, we texted at night after the children fell asleep. My heart pumped thoughts and my brain burst with emotion.

Tammy was about to go on vacation abroad with her long-term girlfriend. We agreed it would be an opportune time for me to explore what was happening with Esther, and for us to examine our own relationship. But, in truth, we already knew.

I felt liberated—after all, that's the beauty of polyamory. Just as Tammy had been free to pursue women while we were together. I'd never been jealous of her, never asked anything of her. I loved her as she was: free-spirited and wild.

"You're a woman with no guarantees," I would tell her, "and that's how you should be loved."

The flip side of this equation was that I didn't need to provide guarantees either. Or so I thought. But feelings are rarely symmetrical, and Tammy was caught unprepared.

She began bombarding me with demanding, disappointed, angry messages. I regarded her like a child throwing a tantrum on the supermarket floor—with compassion, but no intention of yielding.

It took six days from our first encounter on Saturday to our first date at Esther's studio the following Friday afternoon. We couldn't find an earlier time that worked for both of us. While texting to coordinate, she wrote: "I've waited this long, I can wait a bit longer." She also sent: "Elinor, I'm burning hot for you."

Esther, she knows how to speak to me.

Before our first date, I was as excited as a teenage girl, yet I also possessed the quiet confidence of a woman who knows herself. This exquisite combination was only possible thanks to the wisdom that comes with turning forty. We agreed to meet at two in the afternoon, both aware we had three hours together. Tom and the kids were to pick me up at five for dinner at his mother's in Mazkeret Batya. At this stage, he was still living at home; the kids didn't yet know we were separated.

I arrived bearing a jar of homemade truffles and a green wreath fashioned from kale, green onion, lettuce, and arugula—all grown in my urban balcony garden.

When I reached her floor in the graffiti-covered industrial building, she emerged from the studio entrance. She greeted me with a kiss on the cheek, took the green wreath from my hands, and gently laid her hand on my ass. The audacity of this woman, I thought, feels so damn good.

Her studio stunned me. A spacious loft, clean, bright, and airy. Her paintings hung on the white walls—large blue circles, pulsating with radical hope. Opposite the artwork stood a wooden structure spanning an entire wall, housing dozens, perhaps hundreds of canvases. A light leather couch faced this cache of paintings. On the round blue coffee table sat a vase of flowers and small wooden bowls filled with almonds, walnuts, and figs. A glass bottle of whiskey stood beside two ornate glasses.

In the daylight, I was surprised to discover her eyes were blue. "I thought they were brown!" I exclaimed.

"I changed them for you," she smiled. They were just as bright in her face when blue.

We talked endlessly. About our families, about work. She showed me a catalogue of her artwork. We ate figs and sipped whiskey.

I felt at ease, slipping off my sandals to sit barefoot on her couch, clad in jeans and a black tank top.

She excused herself to the bathroom for a moment. Upon returning, she straddled me and began to kiss me. We kissed for an eternity, until she asked, "May I invite you to my bedroom?"

"Yes," I smiled, and she took my hand, leading me after her.

We strode to the bedroom, which looked like a dream within a dream. Some walls were painted black, with paintings adorning every surface. I recognized works by Michal Ne'eman, Pinchas Cohen Gan, Zoya Cherkassky. Wow, I thought, this is the best gallery in Tel Aviv. A solid wood Finnish sauna stood in the center of the room. Next to it, a massive shower gleamed, entirely covered in white epoxy. The bed was elevated, custom-built to fit the space.

On the headboard shelf sat a wide coiled snake, statues, books, two lamps, an antique trumpet, and an old black-and-white photograph of Esther in a striped tank top, gazing directly at the camera. The scent of perfumes misted my senses; I detected lavender and jasmine.

Facing the sauna were black shelves holding perfumes, a vase of flowers, two statues of human-god faces, and large shells serving as jewelry bowls. Above hung a painting of a woman in deep blue and red royal attire, with a crown on her head.

In an instant, Esther was completely naked. I wasn't sure if I'd blinked and her clothes had vanished, or if she was the fastest undresser in history. It took me time to wiggle out of my jeans and top, all while her unfamiliar, arousing beauty captivated my gaze.

She lay naked on the bed, extending her hand to invite me, patiently waiting for my human pace to catch up with hers. Finally bare, I quickly nestled into her arms, slightly embarrassed by the sudden, complete nudity.

There, in her enchanted world, she fucked me like I had never been fucked before.

It was two o'clock in the afternoon when I knocked on her door, bearing a green wreath, a jar of truffles, and clothes on my body. Just before five, we both stepped into the shower, so I wouldn't reek of sex. We devoured each other under the water; I couldn't get enough of her.

As I dressed, moments before leaving the studio, she took a small spray bottle from the shelf opposite the sauna and misted me with floral water that seeped into my neck and stomach. This is how she sent me to Tom and the children waiting downstairs. This is how I got in the car. This is how we drove to his mother's house—the woman who would soon become my ex-mother-in-law. I was dizzy from sex and untamed scents, my hair still damp.

*Posy of Words*

*You came, instantly drawing me to you*
*Bringing me home to the sea*
*From that first moment, I was yours*
*You've been mine for 140 years*
*I bleed deep red upon your white sheets*
*You dye them—our passion now sanctified*

*On shrooms I saw on your face*
*The lines moving with your breath*
*Which you can stop at will*
*For at least nine minutes*
*Because you are life. You are art*
*You are the absolute truth*

*You are girl and boy, woman and wild creature*
*A witch in the deepest and most subtle layers*
*You are a mirror. You are a dream*
*You are one and all with me*
*And all the words combined cannot describe*
*But sometimes this bouquet is all I can offer.*

## Gushing Toward You

We awaken in our Sinai hut after a night of orgasmic starry ecstasy. I guide your hand to my pussy, a tender good morning touch, and you respond instantly. Your fingers, deft and knowing, slip past my underwear to caress my clit. The sheer genius in your touch, my god what you do to me.

We lie together, I'm on my back with you beside me, massaging my clit, feeling how hard I am for you, making me even harder. My hips undulate in feline waves as sweet sounds escape us both. I'm desperate for you to enter me, but you don't—not yet. You tease me with endless circles, tracing around and over my clit, parting my pussy with your fingers, but not entering.

I'm aroused and wet, already begging you. You slide two fingers inside me, then rise from lying to sitting. I spread my legs and so do you, pressing against me, pussy to pussy. One of your hands is in my pussy, fucking-pleasuring, while your other hand is in your own. I watch your spectacular cunt opening, rubbing against my inner thigh. I see your beautiful fingers, which I adore, arousing both your pussy and mine simultaneously. I moan with passion for you.

You're above me, your hair wild, your face beautiful and kissed golden from the mountains. My love for you is infinite and just beginning.

I'm driven wild by everything you do with your hands, you radiance of a woman. You take one of my legs and move it towards you, turning me so I'm half on my side beneath you. One leg straight, you move on it, my other leg bent towards me, leaving me half-twisted, my ass facing you. You continue fucking us both at the same time.

I moan, gasp, sigh, trusting everything you do. 'Whither thou goest, I will go; and where thou lodgest, I will lodge.' Your hips move with their own demand. You're attuned to me with metronome precision, your synchronicity of inner and outer rhythms always moves me. My cunt feels the celebration that is you, responding immediately like a kite to the wind.

I turn fully onto my stomach, and you continue fucking me. The abundance of your fingers, their movement inside me, the unrestrained rhythm, your pussy on my ass—draws howls and yells from me. I muffle them in the pillow so as not to disturb our neighbors in the nearby huts, but you hear and you know.

You speak as you fuck me, softening my soul, composing poems to my pussy with words of passion and lust. I reach between my legs to rub my clit from below, while you fuck my pussy with your amazing fingers and grind your pussy against my ass. I know that my pleasure pleasures you, just as you know the same is true for me. Our sexual intelligence matches too, on top of everything else. You are a living miracle that happened to me. You are the truth, you are a dream.

Your words dance in my ear and enter my heart, while your hands forge new pathways to myself. I come screaming into the pillow. You continue, showing me there's more within me. I believe you, trust you like I've never trusted before, and I come again with loud yells, no longer trying to stifle them. Let the neighbors hear, let them know there are women here who know love.

I finish coming and turn towards you with a Cheshire cat smile. I lie on my back, legs spread wide, and you're above me, strong and magnificent, fucking me deeply again. A stream squirts from me onto your hand, reaching above your elbow. I laugh with release and joy. You look at me with your clear-water eyes and tell me: "More."

You fuck me hard, fuck fast, my legs open and your hand between them. I squirt again.

I'm amazed, emptied yet full in a way I never knew possible. Your eyes sparkle, reflecting pleasure back to me. "I've found the wellspring," you tell me and continue to draw out everything within me.

You coax more and more jets of fluid from my body. You smear my belly and thighs with the waters flowing out of me. We're glistening with sweat and pussy juice and bursting hearts. I am a vessel, finally contained.

You lie down next to me for an embrace, and I run my hand through your hair, now lighter from the sun here. I'm exhilarated by our shared royalty, thinking how everything is enormous yet precisely the right measure, as is everything with you.

We kiss deeply, lips to lips. Beside us, puddles on the mattress.

## Ocean

My love and I recline upon the couch,
Before us, a shell unfurls, a golden eye banishing our fear.
I am her onyx-haired Venus, rising from the sea;
She drops her anchor deep within me,
Laying all of herself inside without hesitation.

We moor, core to core, by the Mediterranean shore.
Colors unfold in my eyes that drink her in;
She's scented with essential oils and Palo Santo,
Her Casablanca tan smooth and wild.
Her breath flows directly to her throne.

She allows me to learn truth within the cavern walls,
In glittering hues as light fractures on her in rainbows.
Together we discover our elasticity,
Our fingers perfectly matched in length,
As the heart's capacity to stretch aspires to infinity.

# Dreality

In the late afternoon, we slip from the galaxy of our own existence into that of humankind. We arrive at the boardwalk, teeming with people, a babel of Hebrew, Arabic, French and English swirling around us. The desire for separation may be national, but the yearning for water is universal.

We reach the sea, shed our flip-flops, and walk hand-in-hand on the sand. Being with you is always romantic—even if we were at a recycling plant watching garbage decompose—but being with you on the beach during a winter sunset, as the sun melts into the sea and the skies blush in pinks and purples, this makes my synapses dance. We revel in the sensation of sand pressing against our soles, its coolness soothing my entire body from bottom to top. Pleasant shivers ripple through me, born of the wind, the cold, or perhaps your nearness.

We stroll along the winding boardwalk heading south and, upon reaching a mosque, we ascend the stairs beside it toward Horoscope Way (Nativ HaMazalot). Jaffa is brimming with beauty, its stones bearing witness to centuries, millennia even. The blood spilled here has long since wept into the sea. She envelops us in the embrace of her stones and I find myself thinking of Jerusalem, the mother in whose difficult and holy womb I was nurtured.

How alike and yet how different they are, these cities where men, in their excess of passion, have piled up bodies. How is it that I've traversed from stone to stone, from sacred to profane?

In my eyes, the holiness of water is more exalted than the wrath of the heavens.

We enter Kdumim Square and walk along the wall of the Armenian church by way of Virgo Alley. A high wall, eaten away by sea salt and crowned with barbed wire, separates us from the strip of blue sea. We descend the slippery steps back toward the beach, holding hands as the narrow walkway spirals down with us. We follow the stairs all the way back to the boardwalk of the old port.

We climb onto the large, flat stones set near the north pier. They're paved between the pier and the water, and we discover a statue of a seahorse carved into one of the stones. We gaze out to sea, where an excursion boat carrying a family of Orthodox Jews races by. The sea is too rough to leave the port, but they apparently don't want to forgo the experience for which they've come to Tel Aviv. The skipper races back and forth within the confines of the harbor, making sharp turns. We hear him yelling in Arabic, and the passengers throwing up from the deck into the water.

From there we walk southward to the fishing area. Amidst the dark testosterone, we let go of each other's hands and walk side by side. In the sporadic market, poor in quantity but rich in aromas, red and yellow plastic crates display sardines, sea bream, blue crabs, red mullets, and calamari. The scent of fish is sharp and determined.

Grandma statues fashioned from giant nets hang on the warehouse doorframes of the port, looking like figures made of enormous stockings. Felt dolls are glued to the walls of a container, dried crab shells attached along the frame of another. I run my fingers over a dried octopus, coral, and starfish adorning the warehouse doors, their dryness at odds with their essence.

On the way to Slope Park, whose popular oxymoronic name is Slope Hill, we pause to look at the sea. Unlike the tamed waters in the port, the waves beyond the promenade fence are wild, splashing salty spray on us with the taste of Mediterranean winter. The crash of waves and white foam breaks against the asphalt in a rhythm of thunderous decibels. A wave party rages just beyond the concrete, and we are its self-appointed guests of honor.

We climb up the hill and settle on the chilly grass. A couple of butch lesbians sit in front of us, sipping drinks from enormous plastic cups. Couples and individuals are scattered across the lawn. People bow their heads to their screens, bluish light flickering on their faces. Their bodies are present before the sea, but their eyes remain fixed on their devices. We look to the sky, discerning colorful threads between the stars, both of us identifying the glittering connections. We see spaceships approaching, which slowly morph into airplanes and then into sharks plowing their way across the sky. They move toward the horizon with their slow tails until they disappear.

# Octopussy

You lie naked before me on your royal bed. I descend to taste your pussy, lingering on the swell of your breasts, your nipples, the softness of your sun-kissed skin. I traverse your stomach, navel, and pubic hair, arriving at your trembling, thrilling flesh—pink, purple, brown, vibrating, burning, complex and enticing. Your pussy is exquisite, the finest octopussy I've ever had in my mouth. I'm in awe, marveling at my fortune—I've won the cunt of a lifetime.

You allow me to pleasure my tongue on your pussy, to gallop across your wildness. I listen to your breaths, attuned to your moans. I focus on your clit but sense you crave motion, so I adjust to you. My tongue dances on you, touching then retreating, maintaining the tension between closeness and distance. It lets you yearn for a moment, returns to you, then again makes space for air.

I breathe over your pussy, whispering words of lust and grace into it. My lips hum above you like a drone of passion. Lips to lips, I tell it how beautiful it is, how much I've missed it. Your ears are distant somewhere above, but you hear me through your pussy. Your flesh absorbs the DNA of my breath from the vapor of my mouth. The vibration created shakes us both.

I slide one finger into your hot cunt, then another. I delve deep into the corridors and chambers of your pussy, exploring every layer that unfolds before me. I know there's so much I've yet to discover. I'm eager to learn, but I'm not rushing.

Fucking you this way ignites me. I rock back and forth on the mattress, grinding myself as I fuck you and whisper-lick your pussy. I grip my orgasm by the mane, holding it back. I'm Tarzan who is actually Jane, swinging between vines of pleasure, roaring my liberation straight from my lungs into your life-pulsing pussy.

I lick you with my nose, my mouth, my chin. If I could, I'd enter you with my entire body, licking through your vulva to your cervix to your fallopian tubes, blowing a hoarse concert into the cavity of your belly. I can't, but I do continue to fuck you deep with my fingers, directing the intensity according to your sounds, your movements, your breath. Your frequencies tune me. You turn me on in every nerve. I can't hold back any longer and I mount you with hot, buttery fucking motions. I scream and you scream with me. We synchronize in vocal spirals to the heavens, until I come on you, howling.

You breathe with me, and then, when I'm entirely wet and soft, you say: "Now I want to fuck you." You rise above me and turn me with my ass toward you. You penetrate me, strong and quick, and I receive you with a satisfied, warm pussy. Grunts escape me. I hear you screaming and hear myself screaming. I tumble in a slalom of pleasure, feeling everything in you as you yell your orgasm into me.

You are my heart's home. Until you, I never knew that this, exactly this, is how you fuck love.

*Forgiving Reality for its Humanity*

*True, I forget to buy tampons*
*And to pick up my son from school*
*That first week of first grade*
*But I'll never forget*
*How he ran to me, love-flooded*
*A gap where his two front teeth used to be*
*Falling into my arms with an enormous grin*
*And I'll never forget*
*How my daughter and I danced together in the car*
*Singing and laughing*
*Rediscovering the channel*
*Back to each other*
*And I'll never forget how it felt*
*To walk through Tel Aviv's most beautiful streets*
*Waiting for you outside your Pilates class*
*To lean against the wall beneath the trees*
*And then to see you emerge from the studio*
*Smiling, sunglasses on*
*How you rode with me on your bike along the sea*
*I, perched on the seat, you standing to pedal*
*My hands on your hips*
*And I knew that now, this moment*
*This, exactly this, is happiness.*

## Soaring Splendor

*In your damp bed*
*Transmuted to a freighter*
*Negotiating between*
*Chocolate and fire*
*We cry out in ecstasy*
*Splitting open the sky*
*In the soul's circuitry*
*We mend childhood's fragments*
*And return the wind to sea.*

## Lick My Walls

All day you upgrade my house. Fixing flaws with putty, painting with roller and brush, you unveil the beauty of the plaster. I work in the rooms, sorting and organizing.

I clear out boxes and bags, keeping only what's necessary, pleasant, sweet. Music plays from a simple speaker—I haven't set up the sound system yet—accompanying our moving hands. Occasionally, I burn sage. Its smoke adorns the air, dancing between us, rejoicing in the feeling of renewal.

I bring you water infused with lemon verbena and mint from my balcony. We move through my house, speaking little, doing much.

I order food to maintain our momentum. We pause with noodles, vegetables, tofu, and fried fish. We silence the music too, listening to each other's quiet.

We don't touch. You hold chopsticks. Your eyes, now grey, lock onto mine, unwavering. Paint stains mark my shirt that you're wearing.

Then we resume our motion, revitalizing the house.

You're precise with the paint. I make trips to the trash and storage. You clean the doors and doorframes for me, I change the sheets on the kids' beds.

You cut a small, precise hole in a rag and wash the floors with a squeegee. Every so often, we pause to admire our progress. Me you, you me, each of us ourselves. Both our hearts are woven into this house, permeating all its spaces.

At midnight we shower and go to bed. I light a diffuser with lavender and lemongrass oils. The grandfather clock chimes twelve times and we return to our original state, naked and close. Your skin is my light. Your touch caresses me down to the foundations.

I lie on you with legs slightly parted, my hand traveling along your hip. Sometimes I pause, exploring an area in depth, absorbing information. With my other hand I brace myself on the mattress for stability, my body in constant motion. My pussy moves slowly in the air above you.

My mouth doesn't stop kissing you. Cheek. The corner of your eye. The ear in all its dimensions. I kiss your neck, lick, suck, moving my hips towards you as you move towards me. My right hand reaches for the opening of your pussy. I linger there, moving slowly, teasing and being teased.

We're both part of the stream now, in the territorial waters of desire. Your pussy invites me in, and I'm drawn into the moonscape unfolding, wet, inside you. My hand synchronizes with my hips above you. I fuck you with my entire body, deeper and deeper, knocking on your heart through your pussy, speaking with the god that is you.

You spray me with showers, sweet waterfalls washing over my fingers again and again. You flip me onto my back and mount me. My body rearranges itself to inhale your cells, to feel you in this new composition. My heart wraps around you, rolling through past lives, through flips from the dawn of history. We've waited all day to unite. We've waited our entire lives.

You sit upright above me, open my legs and enter me with hot fingers. You draw animal screams and wails from me, your pussy open as my eyes gaze at it in worship. My hand grips a blue bar on the headboard as you make me squirt, my heart spilling into your genius hand.

I turn you onto your back, boldly moving to fuck you deeper and faster. Your clit is hard, your pussy soft and warm. This contrast drives my mind wild—this is the pleasure of the wise body, these are the words of a living goddess. "You make me come endlessly," you say, "and this is just the beginning, can you believe it?" Our voices drip. Our caresses span worlds.

You flip me onto my back again and climb on top. "Like a pancake," I laugh, and you tickle me until the laughter erupts into penetration. You know everything. You fuck me through the past into the future. It's a moment in eternity, an eternity in a moment. You explore my multi-shaded pussy, discovering more and more colors in me.

I soar from you, and you take flight with me. Your fingers are the key to the treasure chest you've brought from the ocean depths. You open it, and I explode. I turn you over once more, lie on top of you, and we entwine, talking. I slide to your side, close my eyes, knowing you do the same.

The burning candles flicker as we sink. Our responses to each other slow to a dream-like pace, consciousness loosening its grip. We fall asleep in an embrace that lasts all night and wake to a new house.

# Seeping into Everything

I make plans to go surfing with Dana in Haifa, and you come along. You always enjoy being at the beach, and I've been longing for the two of you to meet.

The surfboard claims the seat next to me, so you sit behind, massaging my shoulder as we drive. We listen to music. The sun is generous, and the sea stretches out like a bronzed hunk to our left. Everything feels so open with you, like a renewed opportunity I've been given.

When we arrive at Bat Galim, Dana is already in the water. She comes out to say hello, and you two embrace as if you've known each other for years. I head into the water with Dana and our surfboards, while you stay behind in your bikini, planning to swim a bit further down the beach.

"Have fun," you tell us. "Have fun," I kiss you, finding it hard to leave.

Two hours later, Dana and I emerge from the water. You're already out, having arrived a bit before us, and you're sitting with Dana's friends who were surfing with us but left the water earlier. Two of them are in their twenties, and two are in their fifties.

I sidle up close to you, filled with an inexplicable longing—it's all the years we weren't together that we need to bridge; we don't have another minute to waste. You want to treat Dana and me, asking, "What would you like? Coffee? Orange juice?" We walk over to the stand together, while Dana sits with her friends to save our spot.

We wait as they squeeze the oranges, our eyes locked on each other. We don't need to speak when our entire essence is laid bare before one another.

Outside, we can hear Dana. She's fighting with one of the employees who thinks she's just a surfer who sat down in their spot. Dana is like a coiled wire—injustice makes her break out in a rash, and all her muscles are poised for attack. When we come out with our cups of orange juice, sparkling water, and coffee, Dana angrily grabs her orange juice, marches back inside, and slams it on the counter. "I don't want your drink," she yells. Another worker calms her down, explaining there was a misunderstanding, and she returns to sit with us.

Dana's friends have already connected with you while we were in the sea. They saw two of your paintings at a museum and are happy to chat. Each of them mentions a friend they know who left her husband and fell in love with a woman. It smells like a trend, and I bristle. "I was with women even before I married Tom," I say, and as it comes out of my mouth, I think to myself—so what. I don't owe them any explanation. They can think whatever they want.

We begin an interesting, inter-generational conversation. One of the younger women tells us about a guy she's dating. "Fucking a man is the easiest thing in the world," one of the older women says. "But it's the only thing that's easy to do with them."

We talk about the great deception, about how young women want to get married, dream of domesticating men, while men just want to fool around. What nonsense, served up on an inverted cultural platter. Every woman around our table, married or divorced, can recount the disappointments with her man, how she became the central axis around which the planet of her world—her family—revolves. The insult of being left alone in the battle. Every woman here, married or divorced, knows how much the man with her needs her, how dependent the children are on her, how she's required to be so much more just to be considered an equal—if not less so. Every woman at our table, married or divorced, can enumerate the difficulties her children's father encounters while raising his own offspring. His incompetence, his mental laziness, his pitiful choices. Each of us knows the cruel shock of discovering that the same brain capable of managing complex systems at work, respected and sometimes even admired by strangers, is a brain that chooses, consciously or not, to be either partially or completely non-functional when it comes to his own home.

'All the glory of the king's daughter is within, lest she embarrass the man with the superiority of her abilities.'

Someone needs to tell the young women that they carry the entire world. Relationships, then parenthood, the home, and work too if they're modern. So we tell them.

We tell them that they carry the beauty, the multitasking, the complexity. They carry children in their wombs, milk in their breasts, work because they need to make a living, they carry the home because it doesn't clean itself, they carry their body in public, mascara on their eyelashes, gel on their fingernails. Appearance and essence.

We tell them that in most families we know, there's one who's responsible and one who's a babysitter following instructions. Lack of responsibility is the biggest privilege of the common married man. We tell them that they're the ones who construct the detailed Excel spreadsheet with after-school activities, carpools, food preferences, school clothing, winter and summer closets, friends, vacations, homework, camp sign-ups, and lactose intolerances. They're the ones in the parents' WhatsApp groups, who find out which after-school activities are good, who are in touch with the teachers and coaches. They're the managers, the implementers, the tooth fairies, and those who don't sleep at night.

The young women ask: "But wait; what. do. they. do???"

I answer, "Well, according to the Facebook group 'Momedy,' which has over half a million Israeli women in it (and it's a wonderful, important, comforting group), the most common nickname for a married man, otherwise known as a husband, is 'The Useless One.' Sometimes they refer to him as 'unnecessary' or 'the toilet seat warmer.' Amusing? Some might think so. To me, it's utterly mama-sad."

"They are the breadwinners," one of the older women says. "They are in positions of power, bring the income, they control the finances. Women may have entered the workforce, but men haven't yet entered the household and, until that happens—women have to do both." The revolution for equality is not yet complete.

We reveal the big secret to the younger women: the men will wither without you. Men have no idea how to exist in the emotional world without you. Men are unable to raise children without you. It isn't because they are incapable, it's because they do not know how to bring their talents to this essential sector. They haven't been trained, prepared, encouraged to do so. And they too lose out in a big way.

"They need you much, much, much, much, much, much, much more than you need them, don't be mistaken."

One of Dana's friends says. "The dream of the white dress is cute, especially if you're eight, but the reality after you have your first children is offensive. The disappointment of discovering how alone you are in this role that has been paved for you is heartbreaking."

Nobody talks about it on social media or in birth preparation courses, so we talk about it in bathing suits, over coffee and orange juice in the sun.

"Men are the ones who are supposed to beg to get married, because that deal serves them a lot more than it serves women."

Dana says. "How it got turned upside down and women are the ones who 'want a husband' is a mystery to me. You can only explain it by internalized oppression and submission, even partially, to the patriarchy that covers every aspect of society, like mold."

When we return to Tel Aviv, the sea to our right, there's a sweet tightness in my muscles and dried salt on my lips.

I put on a calm playlist on Spotify. "Next time, find a way to put the surfboard somewhere else. I want to sit next to you," you tell me.

"As you wish," I answer. As you wish.

# A Husband is Temporary, an Ex-Husband is Forever

It wasn't his fault, nor was it mine. It was simply all we knew. We used each other to plumb the depths of our most putrid shame. We brandished our deepest pain, hoping, trying to heal it together. When we fought, he'd hurl the words I dreaded most. I'd spit back the bitterest truths, unvarnished, without mercy.

We knew no other way to communicate. We only discovered non-violent communication after forty. We fought like playground children—"I'm rubber, you're glue, whatever you say bounces off me and sticks to you." We fought in front of our kids with a blinding, holy rage.

For years, Dana would tell me it was a toxic relationship, that I needed to get out. I'd argue with her.

"He's my anchor," I'd say.

"That's why you're not sailing anywhere," she'd retort.

After the fights came his apology sessions and my tears. He'd say all the things I longed to hear, and I'd open my heart, bringing him back under my wings. Then came the sex. There, we knew how to listen to each other, to forgive, to hold, to learn each other with gentleness and dedication. Then we'd have a few days or weeks of closeness, of understanding. And then another fight, and again, the cycle would start anew.

I thought, and he made sure to confirm it time and again, that no one would ever love me the way he did. That I'd never find anyone who'd accept me like he accepted me.

The fundamental assumption, nestled deep in the pit of my

stomach and carefully nurtured by him, was that who could possibly accept someone as damaged as I was?

After the births, the feeling intensified—with my broken belly and my used-up breasts. But it wasn't really physical. It was a deep-seated feeling belonging to a child who had finally found someone who wanted her, truly desired her. So what if he was a bit fucked up? After all, so was I. So what if he was a little violent? I was difficult too. So what if he was a hopeless workaholic? Nobody's perfect. And that's how the years passed—pregnancies, births, an abortion. Life took root.

"How is it possible, Dana? How did I stay for 17 years?" I asked Dana the day Tom left the house.

She answered: "It's because he fucked you so good, Elinor, remember? The heart in the cunt, that's what decides."

But it wasn't just the sex that held us together. Not the kids either. It was his good, beautiful eyes. It was his arms, his warm hands with long fingers. When my father was dying of cancer and lying in a hospital bed, Tom would visit him every day after work, read to him from his favorite newspaper when he couldn't read anymore because his eyesight was blurry, and would massage his feet. He did it easily, with simple love. During all the births, he held my hands, looked into my eyes, and breathed with me. He had those moments where we knew how to be together, which I remembered, which I will always remember.

And then there was that issue—his tendency to retreat into himself, his self-focus that allowed me to live an exciting life under the radar. Out of our 17 years together, for the last six I had another love, besides him.

He knew about Noga, about Mowgli, and about Tammy Gil. He even met them.

For six years, I outsourced my emotional life.

In the early years, it only rocked our anchored boat more violently, buffeting it from both sides—the growing mental distance between us, and the sex that got better and better. Six years it held, then shattered in a moment—like a cliff face yielding to a gentle tide.

We were on our way back from a trip up north with the kids. We had gone to Mount Hermon to play in the snow. The entire ride he scolded and growled, was mad at them and at me, and I thought to myself: No more. I don't need this.

When we got home, it was a Saturday evening. In our bedroom, I ended it. With all his height, he laid flat on the floor, said, "no, no," bawled, threatened, begged, stopped eating, stopped shaving. Since then, he's gotten over it, and I wouldn't be surprised if he remembers it all quite differently. It doesn't really matter, because this is my story.

At the Rabbinate, I sat in a room with five men who asked us our fathers' names and if they were known by a nickname ("Yes, Yossi"). I had to hold out my hands, and Tom dropped the document into my palms: "In the year five thousand seven hundred and eighty-two since the creation of the world, in the city of Tel Aviv-Jaffa, also known as Tel Aviv, the husband Tom, son of Yehuda, divorced his wife, Elinor daughter of Joseph, with a bill of divorce according to the law of Moses and Israel." Two bearded witnesses watched as his outstretched arm let the piece of paper fall into my hands.

I wonder why it's so important for them to note that it is the man who is divorcing and the woman who is divorced. At this specific fissure, they choose to note who supposedly is breaking up with whom. What is so threatening and scary that they need to play defense proactively, whether they write the truth or whether it is a bold lie. After all, in the newspapers they don't report that the man did the murdering, rather that the woman was murdered.

Women bear tolerance well.

On the steps of the Rabbinate, the mood was muted. We

embraced. We thanked each other. We teared up. We took a picture, hugging each other. It was sad, it was sweet.

Today we are kind of, one could say, friends. Today I appreciate what is, and am less frustrated by what isn't.

His love for the children is epic, his commitment to that love is total. I appreciate that and am grateful to him for the three of them.

"A husband is temporary," Dana taught me, "an ex-husband is forever." As for me, I'm in the business of forever.

## Power Plant

"Maybe you could work from here, from the studio?" Esther asked.

"Great idea," I answered. Most of my staff worked abroad. Most countries had lockdowns, and only Build and Renew was still adhering to the eighties-era policy of 'clocking in.' So fucked. If Tim could work from his kitchen in London and Tony from his living room in Madrid, I could work from Esther's studio in Tel Aviv. One day I simply stopped coming to the office.

I would hop on conference calls on Zoom, made-up, with earbuds, a button-up shirt, and just my underwear below. Behind me, Esther's art stand starred, bursting with canvases. She would cross behind me in the frame wearing a smock or her painter's overalls, serving me green tea and cut-up vegetables. They drank water and ate the cookies Rivka'leh the secretary brought in, leftover from Shabbat. Sometimes they asked me about my background. "This is my home," I would answer, feeling the space within me growing, how I myself was expanding and becoming a container to hold it all.

Yuval, the CEO, called me to order. In a Zoom meeting, of course. "You can't do this," he said, unable to believe this was happening to him.

"Are you satisfied with my work?" I asked. I knew he was, because he'd told me I remembered every detail, that I ticked off tasks at the rate Damien took a toothpick out of his shirt pocket.

"Yes, everything is excellent," he answered. "But you have to understand. All of the company's employees come into the offices. That's the policy here. We have a policy. People can't just do whatever they want."

"Okay," I told him, pleased by him. Yuvali is so good at expressing his desires. Maybe people can't do whatever they want, but that doesn't mean that I can't do whatever I want. I flat-out refused to go in.

I thought they would fire me. I hoped they would fire me. Unemployment benefits and days full of Esther and the beach sounded like a blue dream with a sailboat in the background.

They didn't fire me. I kept surfing, going to Esther's, working from her studio while she painted or cooked or held her meetings, which I sometimes joined out of curiosity, drawn to them like a magnet. We fucked between meetings. We spoke about art, passion, and wine.

On my days with the kids, I drove from her place to home. All at once, the many hours in a day that had been dedicated to unnecessary commutes and constricting small talk opened up for me. I made my own dreamy schedule; I understood that I was the power plant being constructed.

I did that for two months until one day Esther said to me, "Leave Build and Renew. Come work with me."

# Brew and Woo

"Come work with me," she said.

I look at her and smiled, knowing she means every word that leaves her lips.

"Come manage the studio. I want your talents here with me. You've been searching for an escape from your job, from that macho, male-dominated environment for so long. I need to handle so many things, and you'll have time to surf and write. Most importantly, we'll be together all day."

I was yours at 'come,' I think to myself.

We break down the practicalities: what I'll oversee, the financial requirements, the exact steps we'll take.

That same week, I quit my job, informing Yuval of my departure. My contract requires two months' notice, which I declare starts now. He asks me to reconsider, to take on occasional projects. "Maybe in the future," I tell him, knowing there's no chance. The moment I close the door on the old world, I'm no longer there. My gaze is fixed forward and ahead, my horizon shimmering with oil paints and the sea. My kingdom awaits.

Over the next two months, I visit the office every few days, clearing my desk and preparing a folder of Excel files for my replacement. When the two months end, there's paperwork to sign. I return equipment and my laptop, collecting signatures on dotted lines from the head of HR and the company's legal counsel. A modest ceremony takes place in the department.

"Thanks. We've enjoyed working together. Good luck in all your future endeavors. Thank you for your contribution."

"Thank you, I've enjoyed my time here. Thanks for the home I found here." Everyone recites the correct lines.

I receive a chef's grinder and a gift certificate. As I turn to leave, I stand before the elevator, a plant and gift box in my arms, a backpack on my shoulders. *Thank you for what was, thank you for everything I learned here*, I say in my heart without a trace of cynicism, and I step into the elevator, never to return.

The next morning, I wake up to work with Esther. I sit with my laptop amidst her artwork. In the weeks and months that follow, she schools me in the art world and I map it out, placing her within it. I prepare an Excel sheet with tabs, defining status, goals, and milestones. We set up meetings with museum directors, galleries, collectors, art dealers. We work on exhibitions, openings, collaborations, new projects. Her mind is wild and teeming, and I marvel at the many forms that abundance takes.

We hold our most crucial meetings in Esther's sauna in the studio. Seated on the wooden bench, we sprinkle water infused with lavender, tea tree oil and jasmine onto the lava stones. We sweat and talk. Usually, we reach conclusions.

Esther wears a prayer necklace with beads made of lava stones. We go stone by stone, expressing our gratitude. Thank you for abundance, for love, for passion. Thank you for your wise body, for the generosity of your heart. Thank you for the children who exist, thank you for the children who do not. We thank our parents, our siblings. We thank the water, thank the sun. We thank skin, eyes, hair. Thank you for the heat, for sweat, for pores. Thank you for the walls, thank you for the trees. Thank you for the privilege of saying thank you. Thank you for food, thank you for your hands that know everything.

Sweating, we remember grace and give thanks to creation, to the creatress of all that is. We use a cloth to scrub away the skin we no longer need and step out to shower. Afterward, our skin gleams, our souls scrubbed clean. We are prepared for anything that may come.

When Amikam calls to offer me projects, I decline. When I receive an offer from a different engineering company—they'd heard I left 'Build and Renew'—I turn them down as well. *Keep your power plays to yourselves,* I think with relief. *I'm done playing on your court, by your rules. You can save your measuring contests of who's bigger. Mine is the smallest, and I'm the biggest, bitches.*

## Too Much

We were together all day.

We met a friend. We went to a gallery and saw a printer and a telephone receiver flying from an airplane, and Arabic poetry condensing and expanding, the volume reminiscent of the pulsing rhythms at the iconic Allenby 58 dance club in the 90s. The genius of the large industrial space poured out of your fire-eyes. The expanse of blue skies on the enormous screen unfurled in my heart. I overflowed with attraction to you. Outwardly, I showed nothing.

All day we drank coffee, then tea, then coffee again. We talked about Germaine Greer, who argues that equality between the sexes was never a worthy aspiration, only liberation. We spoke about screens and love. Loneliness and connection. Art and boundaries. We touched silk, breathed masks.

We did the weekend shopping. Vegetables, fish, croissants from Michal's bakery—the woman who knows how to whisper to dough. We walked with our arms around each other. You were particularly beautiful in light colors. White pants, a beige jacket, a rockstar straight out of a poster from my wettest dreams. Jim Morrison as a woman, walking arm in arm with me down the streets of Tel Aviv. For once, they were fresh because of the rain, or maybe it was me, my eyes washed clean.

All day long we laid our hands on each other with responsible public decency. I wanted you, I drank you in with my eyes, I behaved impeccably. I was with you all day, and I missed you all day.

We had an eye-opening and screen-lit work meeting with a colleague. You prepared strong, sweet Moroccan tea for us as we solved riddles of access. The two of you ping-ponged ideas back and forth. I sent links. We fine-tuned the uniqueness of a circular emotion, and all three of us couldn't stop smiling. It was pleasant and cool; I stayed wrapped in my jacket inside the apartment.

When the guest left and we were finally alone, you went to the bedroom, and I followed you.

You undressed, leaving only your camisole on. You were untamed and alluring as you know how to be when inviting me to your bed. Your nipples called to me through your top; I felt them harden in my mouth as I moved from one to the other. The sounds you made drove me wild. I got wet quickly but wasn't in any hurry. I licked your beautiful, bold breasts. My pussy's temperature rose between my legs. You asked me to pull my hair back and expose my neck. I did so you could bite. Our body parts flowed to each other as if there could be an end to longing.

We bit, sucked, nursed, inhaled. We growled skin to skin. Breast to mouth, shoulders to shoulders. Bellies kissed, groans ripped from their depths.

My pussy dripped, your golden nipples burned. We ascended in spirals to the goddess of pussies herself. Seconds before my orgasm, I stopped. I wanted to continue feeling the energy, not to come yet. The taste of my pussy was delicious in your sweet mouth. Your lips were soft, inviting, felt like home to me. I kissed you in gratitude.

A kiss for your existence, a kiss for your genius, a kiss for your beauty. I sang your praises in licks straight into your warm, smart pussy. I penetrated you, deep into your heart, and I listened to everything it had to tell me. You came from the depths.

And then again.

Sweaty, in love, we laughed out loud, and petted each other's hair and face. "You're too much!" I said, and you laughed.

"Look who's talking," you answered, and reached out with a confident hand to my pussy.

The things you did to me, the things you know how to do.

God as my witness, I have orgasmed in my life but, like that, I've never orgasmed before. I screamed my orgasm into your ear and all at once you penetrated me. The fountain you found there gushed on your hand. I'll always remember that orgasm, when you turned me into the Nile Delta. From the farthest reaches of myself, from every nerve ending, in one moment I flowed like a river to the sea.

Between the wet sheets, in the deep smell of both of us mixing together, we spoke love. About how we were growing together but also one into the other. We spoke about what cannot be repeated because it is too sacred to be rendered in ink. When we were done worshipping god, you set up a tray for us and we went on to licking things that are not a woman's body.

There is another sex, Yona Wallach was right and, more than that, there is another love. I don't know many things, but I know this is all I want.

## In the Heart of the Forest

*I fuck you as the chief of the land,*
*Crimson core, scarlet pussy.*
*Galloping wild, untamed,*
*Love's eternal vanguard.*

*You fuck me dripping maple resin,*
*In ways only you know.*
*We plunge to the depths of the ocean,*
*Hunting for treasures, launching them skyward.*

*Encircled in your arms,*
*Both souls, sparkle spinning,*
*Our home a stellar cradle,*
*We burst, seeding cosmic life.*

# In a Spaceship

Some ex-girlfriend, for a fleeting moment, sent her hearts on WhatsApp and it stirs my emotions. Faced with the choice to sink or rise, I let my vulnerability surface. In two hours, we'll part for two days and that, too, saddens me. Yet, beneath it all lurks the queen-mother of anxieties—the terror of losing what I have. Shriveled and neurotic, she clucks her tongue, trying to devour morsels of the present.

Lately, I've been shedding people from my life just as I've been discarding unnecessary parts of myself. I remain light, soaring close to the sun. Sometimes, the knowledge that I've won the lottery terrifies me. My love senses everything. She asks me to share. With her serene nobility, she whispers love, anchoring me to her and to this moment.

We retreat to the bed, guarding two hours of eternity. I bring with me the girl afraid of solitude, and the boxer who vanquishes the Ex with a tooth-shattering knockout.

I grab her feet and lick her pussy. Her pussy tastes different every day. One day like chocolate, another day pineapple. Today it has a mango-like scent. There's no explanation for it. It isn't what she eats, it's what my taste buds understand when they read her. I fuck her with my mouth, weak and strong, deep and high. I move with her hips when my mouth meets her sweetness. I drink her in. If only it were possible, I would bottle her nectar and keep it for moments when I miss her.

"Come to me," she calls from above after a time that feels

like a few moments or days. In this spaceship, the laws of time don't exist.

"No!" I say from within her pussy and continue fucking her with my tongue and lips. Her movements, her moans, her heart, rest in my mouth and no ex-girlfriend can touch us now. When she's bubbling over, I add my hand and fuck her with my mouth and hand together. The motion within her synchronizes with my body moving in waves on the sheets. My pussy fucks her through the cock that is my hand in her cunt. Everything is open in the closed shape of infinity.

In this bed, there is the existential fear of a little girl that exists within a mature woman, who remembers that she is the ruler of her kingdom, most of the time. In this bed, there is mango and a dripping pussy and two aliens who set an alarm because soon they will need to say goodbye for two days. This abundance, my god. One could go crazy. The brain cannot comprehend the heights the spaceship is tuned to, so the wisdom of the body takes over, comes to a friend's rescue.

We both wet the sheets and the pillows. I groan into her pussy, she pets my hair. The privilege of being collected into her and the privilege of carrying her on my shoulders are mixed together, exactly like both of our lips in this moment.

I rise up to her. For a moment I feel as though I've been torn away from my beloved pussy, the object of my desire, but I am immediately poured into a new pleasure. I rub my face against her beautiful, warm, feline face. Licking her lips. There are so many worlds in the body, at least as many as the sensations within me.

My hand beats inside her, continues fucking. My breasts in her breasts. "I've never been fucked like this," she says, "I didn't know anything until you." I leave her depths and touch her pussy, rubbing myself with my hand. Both of our pleasure is literally in the palm of my hand. "Turn your hand over," she says, "touch yourself and I'll rub against you." I do it.

The possibilities for playing with her are endless. The fucker is fucked. There is no gender and no age, only discovery and feeling. With bare hands and pounding hearts, we carve paths to eternity.

I turn her over to fuck her from behind. Her ass makes me dizzy, my pussy wets her. How can she be both solid and liquid at the same time? Her back is beautiful and strong, my desire no less. I've long since gotten rid of my fear, I'm naked of it, galloping towards my love like a savage toward his love. We moan, pound. I give to her and she gives in to me. "Finish with me?" she asks.

"Now? Are you close?" I ask before I am about to explode.

"Now," she says, and I go over the cliff with her.

The orgasm momentarily blinds me.

After the screams quiet down, I discover that the fear is gone. It evaporated in the simmering of our bodies. We're left with a concentrated axis of falling in love, even closer than we were two hours ago. Her eyes are grounded in me. My heart beats with the knowledge of our togetherness. I can leave her now. I know what's important. Another unnecessary layer has been shed.

## Terra Incognita

She is revered, an uncharted land, an uncrackable enigma. She is both the riddle and the answer to questions I never knew I was asking. Her essence permeates every part of me. She moves between ventricles and atria, her bare hand wielding a tube of paint, adorning the walls of my soul.

To decipher her, one must gaze upon her as one does the sun, with naked eyes. It's an impossible feat.

Her age is impossible to guess, and there's no need to try. The year of her birth is scattered across the internet like a meaningless combination of numbers. Dozens of people, who brought dozens more she didn't know, showed up to the birthday party she threw at her studio. A young woman, an art student, stood transfixed before one of her paintings for long minutes before saying, "I could live here." Her mouth agape, moved beyond words. She might as well have said, "Fuck me." Esther looked at her silently, buttoned the top button of her shirt, turned around, and clung to me.

She could seclude herself in her studio for days on end, emerging with paint lodged in the crevices of her fingernails, her overalls stained. She'd shower off the scent of turpentine, dream of oil paints in the night, only to return to the studio the next day to birth more creations.

She swirls with reality, pedaling her eternal bicycle through the horizontal city—to the sea, to the organic shop, to the café, to the bar. Her determined, wild heart beats in time with Tel Aviv.

She's of the sea, she's of the spirit. She is mine as much as she can be anyone's; but truly, at the core of things, she belongs to painting. She swore to be a painter at six and has never been anything else. Painting surrounds her on all sides, flows through her veins. It is her parent, her teacher, her healer. It is solace and knowledge. It is her element and she is painting. They are not truly separate. She serves it and it materializes through her. Her tubes of color are the tools. The paintings—prayer.

She contains contradictions the way others pretend to have consistency, their fixations a mask for anxiety. She fears nothing because she has already been saved from hell and survived it.

Time itself arrived for her and, instead of passing through her, as it does for all of us, it gently encircled her and continued forward, to ordinary people. She is immersed in the radiance of the divine, as inviolable as the sage Honi who drew a sacred circle around himself. She is blessed by eternity; with a working hand woven with veins she guides her fingers through oil paints and gives birth to life through them.

Like her paintings, she looks different from every angle. At twilight she glows golden. She is mountain-tanned, she is wisdom from other worlds. She can't be domesticated, cloned, cultured, owned. She isn't tamed, a wild horse, a human cheetah. She is pure like the water she pours from a clay jug, all her words are truth, all her intentions poetry.

From the day we met I have been learning her, and I always understand only a specific angle. From different angles she is a totally different person. Somehow the whole collage makes sense.

Physical experiences, bounded ones, do not define her. "You can be afraid and happy on the same surface," she paints and says. The horror that runs through everything, oh the sweet horror, is just another material allowed to her.

She is a memory alchemist, turning movement into material in space. Her physical movement creates mental movement, an expanding experience beyond human communication. It's intergalactic communication, out of the star that she is, making a connection with the star that I am. The animal and the divine switch between us, turn over, dance (like gender, like identity, like belonging). When she tears into a croissant, I can cry from the precision with which she moves her hands.

She reminds me to trust the universe. The path that is revealed and revealing. She tells me about creating something from nothing and about the magic of providence. In the meeting of the volcanic eruption of emotion with her absolute control over matter, she reveals to me the wonder of the momentary, the infinity that can be touched at the edge of every moment.

# Never Stop

You smell of Moroccan oil, your hair gleaming. Your body is my favorite among all bodies. Tears well inside me, unspilled, clouds gathering in my belly. Steamed sensitivity served on a bed of sweat and white sheets.

My body clings to you but hasn't yet fully opened. Your fingers are genius upon me, then within me. Many women inhabit this bed. The one liberating herself from patriarchy. The one shedding a corporation from her skin. The mama bear. The little girl with bangs and ponytails in a dark burgundy sundress. And you, the rockstar, spreading through all of us like oil paints on linen canvas. Penetrating every particle of me in liquid silence.

I approach your soft, strong belly and kiss it. I kiss slowly. Kiss your pelvic bones. Your thighs. Your skin that I long to sink into, to dive into you like a pool of molten chocolate. You offer me your pussy, your hips dancing, and I lick it. My mouth grows wet from you, your pussy wet from me. You brush my hair aside and we lock eyes, mouth on pussy, gaze meeting gaze, lips upon lips.

You ask me to rise so you can taste your pussy from my mouth. I come up, and we lick together. "My pussy is sweet," you say, "and salty. Sweet from missing you, salty from the sea you brought."

I move over you in waves as you insert clever fingers directly into my sweet, salty wetness.

We fuck, moan; I grasp your head, your hair, wild with passion and my heart's expanding boundaries. "Please," I beg, "Never stop fucking me. Stay inside me forever."

"I'm staying here all weekend," you answer, "staying inside you." I ride you until a long, insane orgasm coils out of me in screams. The love valve opens within me; you know exactly when to flip me onto my back and make me squirt geysers. We are drenched.

Since the beginning of time, you've drawn me to you, and I, in my brilliance, agreed to come. Or perhaps I called to you, and you, in your genius, knew how to listen. Either way, it keeps happening, again and again. Infinity. The shape of our ring.

You fuck me with all your might and come on me hard. And then again. And again.

You fuck me like no one else. Strong and burning, the sun of my life. We fuck more and more, becoming animals and then back to women. We stop because we run out of time, not because we are finished.

You are in tears. I'm on top of you. You don't need to say anything because I know, but I'm glad that you do. You are the smartest nonchalant I've ever met.

When the heart cracks to widen, crumbs fall. As it stretches, visible fissures appear, neck thrown back.

How sweet and deep it is. An abundance of love is upon us like manna from heaven, and its taste is like a drop of honey.

*Oh Babe*

My babe is the hottest thing in the universes
We peel off our clothes and drunkenness
I lick her pussy with wet hunger, passion drenched
I lick and cum, lick and moan, lick until my thirst is quenched.

My babe is the smartest I've ever seen
An aesthetic pilot on a fossil fuel engine
She's the tribe genius, a naughty boy, alien queen supreme
She kneads awareness, kneads my body 'til I scream.

My babe outshines the Northern Lights
Her x-ray vision reveals full nudity under the fight
She stitches fears between silent spaces
She penetrates, unravels doubt's traces

## Living on a Boat With You

Living on a boat with you is a cradle's asymmetrical rocking. It's getting tipsy before my lips even graze the wine glass, misty-eyed from sunsets so beautiful they look like posters in a travel agent's window—too perfect for the mind to fully grasp.

Living on a boat with you is savoring salt-flavored kisses from your captain's lips. It's feasting on fish and salads, then flushing the toilet straight into the sea, for the fish to feed on us.

Living on a boat with you is noticing every movement, moving in perfect synchrony. It's descending the stairs with care as the boat perpetually sways. It's minding my head, guarding my shin that I persistently bang on the way up.

Living on a boat with you is the quiet born of monotonous rituals. Before sleep, you raise the bridge, I extinguish the candle on deck. It's listening to wood creaking, knowing the boat is old and wise, and we are guests in her warm womb.

Living on a boat with you is dwelling in the waters of passion. It's an '80s mirror in solid wood furniture, it's the love boat—a vessel cradling love within love that cradles a boat.

# You Drank the Sun

I return to her after four days by the sea with the children. We embrace. Kiss. She prepares vegetables and crafts a root salad. She's all about nourishing me. We discuss the essential things, distilling essence into tasks. We open notebooks and write. When our breathing settles, she says: "Come to bed." We undress in the glow of a red lamp. Two tanned bodies that can't exist without the sea.

We've yearned for each other. We cling together and, as always, I'm a furnace against her skin. "You've swallowed the sun," she tells me.

I part my legs instantly, and she plunges into me. It's intense. I gush and gush, soaking the bed with my cunt's fluids. "You've brought the entire sea with you," she says, coaxing more from me.

I gaze at her. I know her soul, and she's the most exquisite creature I've ever beheld. "I'm a woman who never squirted before you," I remind her of what she already knows.

"You're the treasure I discovered at sea," she says, "and I possess the key to your chest."

I'm on my back, she folds my leg, and I'm completely twisted, devouring her with my eyes while offering her my ass. Hyper-flexible joints are a blessing in bed. Her wetness paints the inside of my thigh. She fucks me, and I cry out. I see her, the ceiling, then nothing as I close my eyes, only to snap them open wide when I come.

She flips me over completely, inserts the double-sided dildo into herself, then fucks me from behind. She screams and so do I, our cries expressing what our bodies can't process any other way.

Mid-fuck, she tosses aside the dildo and penetrates me with her fingers. I'm lost in a whirl of colors, her finger anchoring me like a keystone. I focus on the connection between her hand and my body. I come again.

"I'm so open for you," I tell her.

"My love, you're so open to me and you are so beautiful," she replies. She fucks me until she comes, her screams pouring into me.

She grabs the dildo again and lies down. I sit on her, back straight. I hold her and she holds me. She grips my hips, cups my breasts. I grip her hips, cup her breasts. Each moment brings variation. Every instant holds the possibility of change.

She reaches out, her fingers playing with my clit, and I'm going wild. I hover on the edge of orgasm for what feels like eternity. "If you come, I promise I'll come with you," she says. I'm close. I ride long and deep on her beautiful cock and cunt. I want more of this moment. Don't release. The orgasm pulls me onward and I fly forward. I come in a long, unbroken chain, and she joins me, coming as she promised.

We melt into each other's embrace, and I spill with her into the night.

## Amphitrite and Aphrodite

She who emerges from the sea trails long hair in her wake, shedding strands of brown and silver like expired vows. Paths between then and now litter the floor, the mattress, the bathtub. Her body arches in wave-like motions, a vestige of her sea-creature origins—Amphitrite, who once danced in Atlantis' currents.

Her love surged from the sea's cold belly, ascending eleven kilometers from the depths to join the brazen water lilies as they waltzed with plankton and crabs, basking in the warm sun. Salt residue lingers on her lips, her skin perpetually sun-kissed, even in winter.

She who descends from the sublime moves with certainty, sculpting dimensions from silence, illuminating the eternal from within. With precise hands, she carves statues of light in the air, crafts exquisite pastries, and coaxes lovers to ecstasy. She freezes moments suspended in the illusion of space, conducts an orchestra of colors, and triumphs over human definitions with knockout grace.

Her freedom shatters conventions, is infectious. She's a leader who doesn't look back, doesn't count likes, only plays games she loves. She's blazing hot, warming with her energy burners, firm yet soft from an abundance of saunas and wisdom.

They lie together, she of the sea and she of the divine, beginning to intertwine. Their movements imprint the mattress with scents of prey and home, of skies and sand. Their screams are absorbed by the sheets; the silence between screams is deceptive—overflowing and thick.

Tears stream down the cheeks of the one from the sea. She opens and closes. It's sweet and thick for her, and bitter. The one from the divine holds her, pins her close, and whispers directly into her ear, next to the running tears.

The sea-born moves her hips, clinging in cascading waves, her body translating the words flowing from her lover's lips. The divine one meets her and, in her generosity, gives, gives, gives.

She of the sea spreads her legs, wetting them both. She cries and wets, cries and wets. The divine one doesn't relent until she has sprayed all of herself, until she is spent from coming.

The pain and joy seep into the mattress, becoming a permeating puddle. It has no taste, no smell, but it holds oceans' depths of intelligence. One skilled in deciphering could learn the sea's treasures from it.

They are quiet now, holding each other like a moment pinching time, like the ocean catching the sun. A stain spreads, penetrating the mattress to its core. It will take days to dry.

## All the Words That Drip from the Corner of My Mouth

I love your sweat
How your voice meets your teeth
Those lips whose essence is to love
What they, in their impudence, know to stir in me

I love your soft skin
That flows beneath my hands when I glide over it
The chocolate aroma of your cunt
The taste-of-home in my mouth

I love your eyes that shift colors
The strength and precision in your movements
Sometimes my heart swells and tears rise
From how your hands dance when you speak

I love your gentleness when you're
Unraveling the tangled barbed wires of the soul
And the roughness of the wild mare that emerges
When you reject bullshit and shallow people

I love your playfulness
The mischievous smile that bursts from you like an amused boxer
I love the wisdom of the years you have over me
And how you truly have no age or boundaries

I love the queen bee that you are
You're an alpha female and sometimes an alpha male
I love that my list of love for you is infinite
And I've only just begun to tell you what I love.

# When it's Hysterical, it's Historical

I'm sitting on your couch, crying. My skin is as thin as baking paper forgotten in the oven. One light touch of a finger and it will crumble. I'm left a slug, defenseless against the falling tears. I want to speak but this lump in my throat, it won't let me.

You look at me with eyes that know how to change colors and guide me slowly, gently, generously, towards a conversation.

You ask how much I'll allow you to be with me in the pain. How deep I'll let you penetrate. I answer that I consent more than I ever have before. I trust you because you are all truth.

You tell me what you see. A girl who is hurt, wounded. "When it's hysterical it's historical," you say, and I feel more naked before you than when we're undressed. I tell you about that childhood pain of not being seen. Or heard. The one who was yanked between countries and houses, who no one stopped to talk to.

You listen with the smartest eyes I've known. You listen as your hand pets mine. I feel like an abandoned toddler suddenly picked up. We sit together on your couch, cradling the child I was. "Be her mother," you say, "there's no other mother."

Later in bed I ask you: "Fuck me." You grasp me tightly and penetrate me. All at once, everything makes sense. What is it in your fingers that allows me to breathe? The holiness of the universe concentrates in the connection between your hand and my cunt. I've never been more religious than in this moment.

You fuck me wildly and I move against you as if I'm about to break. I growl, roar, climb high. I cling to you, hurling myself on the seam between water and land, where waves shatter into white foam. Your hand is the only thing that makes sense now.

Suddenly, I spill over. You are the ruler of my waters. You hold me with me from within, extracting the corks of secrets begging to be revealed. A stain in the shape of the Sea of Galilee seeps through the layers of the mattress and reaches the bed's base. Oh, my Sea of Galilee, were you ever there, or was it a dream? How many prayers, how many love songs have been written to the silvery vision, squirted by God herself.

After I've made the bed wet, I turn you over, lie down on you. Your mouth is beneath me, open before me like an exposed pussy. Your teeth are perfect. When I'm on the edge of coming, you tell me: "If you come, I'll fuck you so good." You say it from the depths of your warm, moist mouth, and I have no choice but to come on you, screaming.

You always keep your promises and fuck the shit out of me. From the front, from behind, my ass pressed against you, trembling on you, vibrating against you, finishing you inside me.

## You Came

*You came and plucked me from the sun*
*Amidst a crowd, I sat utterly alone*
*A wild spirit in a world of cocaine-dusted faces*
*Playing with all, yet not part of their game*

*You rode in on a bicycle, then stopped*
*Locked it and strode straight toward me*
*Sat down next to me and said: "Thank you for waiting"*
*You, with those eyes of yours*

*"Yes, I was waiting," I answered. "Thank you for coming"*
*We resumed our 140-year conversation*
*I remembered I was never truly alone*
*You wanted, so you arrived; I believed, so you came.*

# Space Doesn't Need the Sun to Acknowledge It

You're sitting on the couch in my living room. An old, white horse lies on its side, resting upon you, its head nestled on your thigh. As you stroke its mane, you suddenly say, "She's too heavy for me," then turn to her and urge, "Yalla, get up." She tries, kicking with her hooves, but she's heavy, limp, unable to rise. You extricate yourself from beneath her, stand up, and brush off your pants. She remains sprawled on the couch, eyes wide open.

A field of babies unfolds before us. Thousands of naked infants appear in neat rows. There are babies who resemble grumpy old men—wrinkled and unsatisfied, their mouths curved downward, quick to break into tears—but not these. These are arranged in lines like toy soldiers, identical in form but varied in size. Their genitalia are neutral, genderless. All are bald with big eyes and penetrating gazes, fixed on us. As we look, they multiply, thousands becoming tens of thousands. "They send shivers through all my senses," you say, reaching for my hand.

The babies' greed dissipates as I turn to you. We're seated on a porch in the southern Golan Heights, the Sea of Galilee stretching below. You transform into an ancient turtle, 250 years old. In some turtle species, certain organs—lungs, liver, kidneys—never age. With you, I think, it's your curiosity and sense of wonder that remain eternally childlike.

Gazing toward the horizon, I see stars conversing, twinkling in Morse-like signals, gossamer lines of light pulsing between them. Suddenly, I grasp that everything communicates with everything else—how foolish to think anything in the universe is inanimate.

You tell me I am an Indian chief watching over you. Be sure of it, babe. "We were together 140 years ago, from the same tribe," you tell me, and I immediately know it was the Lakota. "We were lovers, very young, and we couldn't get married. You were the chief's son, destined to marry another, but we never stopped loving each other."

I see the 17-year-old Indian girl you once were—braided hair, young and innocent. We've loved through all these years, through countless incarnations, always searching for a way back to each other. It's so clear.

I think about recognition, the desire for others to see and say how wonderful, what a good job you did. The longing for applause, how we all project our needs on each other. To be seen. To be accepted. To express ourselves. I understand the limitations of my skin that contains my infiniteness. Space doesn't need the sun to acknowledge it. I will expand to infinity, for it is my essence, and I will reveal you as long as breath fills me. This too is my essence.

Diamonds and demons collaborate in the field below, tumbling toward the Sea of Galilee in an exuberant game of tag. Our diamonds and demons—what would we do without you?

"Aesthetics," you say, "is part of the Zen principle whereby perfect execution leads to spiritual elevation and enlightenment." You have no choice but to worship it. Aesthetics is your ethics. It's your role to discover beauty in the world. Suddenly, I understand everything.

## Fucking Fabulous

We made love and the pain burned until it melted away. You entrust me with the one thing no one else can have—your surrender. You're learning to let me give to you, and I am a dedicated student of your cues.

We stretched out time slowly. "Like the way I draw," you said. "Paying attention to everything."

Slow and deep, we drew each other, one inside the other. You enchanted a path for me along the edges. We had hot and sweet conversations without words. We came together, hard, at exactly the same beat—the most in sync we've ever been. The most united two woman-beings could possibly be. When we're high in spirit, one hundred percent body, this accordion holds all the notes.

Afterward, we showered, drank coffee, and then you fucked me on the kitchen table. I asked for you from behind. I lay on the table, legs spread, ass lifted toward you. Sometimes I need you so much, sometimes this is the only way I know. Like the sunrise, you brought the sun straight between my thighs.

You wondered if the passersby could see us from the window. I couldn't care less if they saw, I didn't give a damn. Nothing mattered to me except you.

When we left for the subway, I felt my legs shaking a little. Stability became spaghetti, my pussy no less excited than my heart. How is it possible that love like this exists, we wondered. This is lionhearted happiness, it is. It is above and beyond all dreams.

"What did I do until you came?" you asked.
"You waited for me," I answered. "Like I waited for you."
"I waited longer." You smiled at me.
I gripped your fingers tight in mine. I'll never let go again.

# My Eldest Daughter

You're 14, and it's your first time in Sinai. Esther and I brought you, along with your younger sister and brother. Ten days without internet. Ten days of moonlight shimmering on water and sunsets painting the mountains. Ten days of turquoise seas and pink-red peaks, of straw huts and meals twice a day.

In the mornings, you'd crawl into our bed, acting out scenes from a book we brought. You were Yertle the Turtle, your sister a rabbit, and your brother an ever-changing cast of characters. Our days consisted of plunging into the water, eating, playing backgammon and cards, more swimming, reading, another dip in the water, another meal. As night fell, we'd gaze at the stars before drifting off to sleep, only to wake and repeat it all again. A routine with a broad-hearted horizon, a primordial reminder of life before wi-fi.

Directly in front of our hut, a straight line into the deep water, lies the entrance to the reef. It's a magnet for divers from our camp and the neighboring ones. It took me days to grasp the reef's depth and structure, to understand where the shallows gave way to deeper waters and then to the vast reef beyond. With each snorkeling expedition, I ventured a little deeper, a little farther—sometimes with Esther, sometimes with each of you kids—until I discovered the gateway to the great coral reef. Oh, the blue that unfurled there! At eight meters deep, fish flaunted colors that only LSD and shrooms could comprehend. Blue, purple, and yellow shells opened and closed like smiling pussies. With your siblings, I stayed near the reef's entrance, wary of the depths beyond. But with you and Esther, I delved into that ancient, underwater splendor.

It's our final day here, ten days of boundless freedom drawing to a close. The sun rises at five, and I'm already awake. Esther is asleep in our hut. You're up early too, your siblings are still sleeping. We meet outside, facing the sun as it emerges from the sea. Here, it becomes clear why the Torah was given at Mount Sinai. Divinity sings from every atom. Forty years of wandering, and I'm certain they never grew accustomed to these colors.

I ask if you're interested in one last dive. We're leaving Sinai at ten but, if we go now, we can make it. You challenge me, "Are you brave enough to go in the cold water?" Then you add, "I'll go in if you do." I fetch our snorkels.

Only with you do I dare venture into the sea's depths. You're 14, taller than I am now. You've won medals in city-wide swim competitions—second place in fifty-meter breaststroke, third in fifty-meter freestyle. As a sea scout, you understand winds, knots, and currents. When you were little, for Purim you dressed up as Ariel, the Little Mermaid, for three consecutive years. I got the message, and everyone knows: you may live on land, but there's no doubt you're a child of the sea.

We enter the water. It's so cold that I freeze when it reaches my hips. You ask, "Mom, do you want to give up?" Those words—give up—when they follow "Mom," are unbearable.

We decide to jump in all at once. Take a deep breath and plunge. For one frozen moment, the body is shocked, but then it's immediately pleasant. It's surprising how not cold it really is. It's always so strange, the gap between what we anticipate and what actually happens.

We swim and swim, making our way to the reef. The quiet here is birthed by divinity. I hear my breathing inside my snorkeling mask—existential, meditative sounds. Inhale, exhale. Inhale, exhale.

Here and there we spot fish, gray in the shallow waters. The tide is low in the mornings, so the water remains shallow for a long stretch. We keep swimming, occasionally pointing out a fish so the other can notice it. A thumbs-up—I saw it.

We reach the deep area, then deeper still. The blue intensifies, the turquoise more vibrant than ever. Before entering the reef, there's a sea anemone with two clownfish. You've always paused here on our snorkeling trips; you love these Nemo fish. You once told us, "They're so sweet, always together in a pair, and they have a house they never leave." We linger for a moment, observing the striped monogamous fish, then continue inward. When the reef opens up, it's dazzling. Beneath us, a school of black fish glides by. My heart flutters at the beauty. We smile at each other through our masks.

We swim through the opening to the other side, to the reef wall. Just as we cross to the deeper side, a school of tiny fish appears before us. They're small, metallic, glittering blue. They keep coming, and it takes me time to grasp the enormity of this school. At first, they're ahead of us, then they surround us, more and more all around. I check with you to confirm you're seeing this too, double-checking that I'm not hallucinating. We're at the center, and they encircle us completely, 360 degrees. I reach out for your hand as thousands, maybe tens of thousands of little fish swirl around us, electric in their beauty. A perfect circle, blue, shining, twirling more and more, and we're hypnotized, clasping each other's hands. It's one of the most thrilling sights I've ever witnessed. The sea knows how to bestow such grace.

I know it's in your honor, my sensitive sea girl. I know the sea recognizes you as part of itself, and I'm awash with gratitude for the privilege of being here with you.

Eventually, the fish depart, their school moving on to bless another place. We surface and remove our masks to talk. "Wow, I've never seen anything like that," I tell you.

"Right??" you say-ask.
"Wow!" I repeat.
"Wow!" you echo.

We replace our masks and submerge our heads, but I no longer see the reef. I realize we've drifted too far, and I abandon my plan to swim along the wall. "Let's go back," I say immediately.

You respond, "Yes, we should. There's a current, the sea is pulling us in."

I see nothing but blue all around us, so I start swimming toward the beach, using our hut as a marker for the reef's entrance. I swim, move, make progress forward, and then a wave comes, breaks, and pulls me back. For every stroke forward, it drags me back two. My heart begins to race.

I look for you and see that you've been swept out, now a few meters behind me. I don't like it, but I trust you. You're an excellent swimmer and a strong girl. Each of us must give our all now.

My breaths grow heavy and constricted inside my mask, and I feel starved for oxygen. I lift my head above water and remove my mask for a second to take a deep breath. The waves are breaking exactly where I am, spraying water on my face. I replace my mask, fearing water might enter my throat and make breathing even harder. I swim and am pulled back, swim and am pulled back.

During Luna's birth, my middle child, after two and a half hours of floating in the pain of contractions, there was a moment when I understood that now I needed determination. Either I give it my all, push like hell to progress the birth, or I could get stuck for hours and exhaust myself. In the water with the waves toying with me, I remember that moment of choice. I recall, too, that people drown when they're exhausted, and I understand that I need to give everything I've got while I still have the strength. I charge forward, breathing heavily in my mask, swimming stronger, harder.

I see you behind me, fighting the waves at the same pace as I am. I don't know what to do. I don't want to let myself drift back to you because then we'll both be too far out, but I don't know what I'll do if you can't get closer to me. I push those thoughts aside for now. I have a plan: reach the reef wherever I can, grab a piece of coral, then give you a hand and pull you to me.

I can't reach the reef's entrance, but I see it getting closer. I touch the coral for a brief second before the sea pushes me away. I swim even harder and manage to grab a piece of the coral growing on the reef wall. It's rough and thorny, but I don't care. I cling like a frog to the reef itself, gripping the coral tightly with one hand as waves crash me against it.

I see you coming closer and hold out my hand, but you can't reach. You're still too far, but nearer than before. I watch you getting closer with your strong strokes, then see how the sea pulls you back. You approach again, I stretch out as far as I can. You almost touch my hand before the sea yanks you away once more. You come closer, your fingertips grazing mine, and the sea drags you back. With every wave that rattles me, I clutch the coral with all my strength. I feel myself being cut, but I focus solely on your hand, which needs to reach mine. You catch another wave, it brings you to me, and this time I grab you.

We cling to each other. You break free from our grip and swim beside me to the reef's entrance. There, with a few movements, you enter the safe, calm area where there's no current. In a few strokes, I join you. I notice my heart is pounding at a frantic rhythm.

I pretend to be calm for your sake, as if what happened was just a bit stressful and I knew it would be fine all along. As if I hadn't just confronted my most primal fear. We lift our masks to speak above the water's surface.

"I was nervous," you tell me, "so I sang myself songs in my mask."

"My wonderful girl," I say to you, "My sea warrior!" I'm so happy I cry tears of relief. They mingle with the sea.

We swim back to the beach, pausing by the pair of clownfish and their dancing anemone. You point at them and we smile at each other under our masks. I give you a thumbs-up, as if to say I saw, while my heart still clenches in my chest. We keep swimming toward land.

When Lev, your little brother, can't find something, he says that he has 'losed it lost.' How lucky that we weren't losed lost or, actually, the luck is that we were found. My breath slowly calms in my mask, inhale exhale, inhale exhale.

Esther is waiting for us on the beach, pacing back and forth like a mother goose. "I woke up suddenly, in a panic," she says. "I realized you were in the water. I was worried about you guys, I had a bad feeling." She wraps each of us in a towel and a hug, then the three of us embrace together. I don't want to cry in front of you, so I take her aside and tell her what happened. My thigh is bleeding, so is my stomach and so are my fingers, places that rubbed against the rough reef.

We go to take a shower. The bleeding stops, but I'm left with marks. There are red lines down my thigh, as if a bear claw swiped at me, a sign from nature reminding me what transience is.

At breakfast, our bags are already packed, and we're waiting for the taxi that will take us to the border. There are whispers around us, and I go to find out what they're talking about. At the beach north of us, at exactly the same time we were out at the reef, a father tried to save his two children who were in the water. He managed to push them out of the current, but he himself did not survive. When they pulled him out of the water, he was already dead.

I put my fork down on the table. I can't eat.

## It's in the Look

The opening of 'Rasmia Barbur' was a vibrant spectacle. Music pulsed from the DJ's decks as an endless stream of small plates flowed from the kitchen. Ram and his partner Gidi strutted about like preening peacocks, all smiles. A dark green wall served as a canvas for climbing plants, while the bar's clean lines echoed the bench installed along the opposite wall. Bamboo hues melded with soft lighting, bartenders worked tirelessly, and we couldn't stop grinning.

Ram, a friend of Esther's, owns several establishments: two restaurants, three bars, and a café. He's razor-sharp, flirtatious, and generous and, like many others, has a fondness for the sound of his own voice. Unlike many in his profession, Ram is sober. He doesn't touch drugs, light or heavy. He clinks glasses merely to please his guests, but I suspect he relishes being the only clear-headed soul among the intoxicated. 'Blessed stumblers,' he calls those who drink so much they can barely walk out the door.

Ram is married to Nadia, a Pilates instructor, and they have two little girls. He returns home at five in the morning, showers, then prepares breakfast for his daughters. After dropping them at preschool, he finally sleeps. He wakes in the afternoon, works out, and collects the girls from preschool. As they prepare for bed in the evening, he departs to visit his establishments.

As in many bathroom stalls in many venues in Tel Aviv, white powder made its star appearance in his places too. Here, as elsewhere, people emerged from stalls sniffling, hungry only for alcohol, not food. (I got it: in restaurants, you sniff after the main course; in bars, the tab is open. Cocaine and alcohol are best friends and, as we know, you don't separate best friends.)

Ram abstains from gluten and sugar, running almost daily. He dyes his hair to conceal the white, and rumors of his nocturnal adventures with women have reached us too, only to dissipate like the cigarette smoke outside his restaurants.

Shirley, Esther's brilliant friend, is an architect and interior designer. By some cosmic coincidence, Esther is surrounded by architects. Perhaps it's their shared sensitivity to space, or their intimate relationship with aesthetics; whatever the reason, they orbit her.

Esther and Shirley's friendship, forged years ago, runs deep, transcending time and space. When Esther and I first met, Shirley welcomed me with open arms, and I immediately felt at ease with her. She exudes a calming quietude and effortless cool, mirrored in the spaces she designs.

When Ram found himself entangled with a designer who repeatedly failed to deliver, he sought Esther's recommendation. She introduced him to Shirley. They began collaborating, and Shirley, as honest as Ruth Bader Ginsburg and as graceful as Lady Di, conjured up a bar of unparalleled magnificence for him.

"Have you seen the bathrooms yet?" Michal, Shirley's partner, asked us. "You should," she added.

Few bathrooms come with personal recommendations, so we turned our attention to them. At the far end of the rectangular space, Shirley had constructed a gallery—a second floor reached by a black iron spiral staircase—which housed the two bathroom stalls.

We gazed down at the crowd, soaking in the pleasant atmosphere infused with the excitement of a new venue's birth. We marveled at Shirley's ingenious idea to raise the gallery, effectively doubling the space while maintaining its airiness.

The bathroom stall opened with a pocket door that glided

on its track with Japanese silence. We scrutinized every detail: the perfect black handles, the quiet closing of the door, the pink princess philodendron perched on the shelf above the flush tank.

As we emerged together, a man waiting outside gaped at us in astonishment.

"He thinks we were fucking in there," I said to Esther.

"He thinks we were doing coke," she replied.

We descended and rejoined our friends, confirming that indeed, the bathrooms were impressive. Shirley and Michal's sons, both soldiers, had arrived with their girlfriends, as well as sweet Gali, Nissan, and Dominique. Friends from various circles warmed our hearts, accompanied by wine and sushi rolls that kept emerging from the kitchen. We danced, and Esther showered me with kisses. She whispered in my ear that I was beautiful, "I see all the wildness in you," she said. Her hands caressed my ass, tightening around my hips.

Being close to her intoxicates me without any mind-altering substances. Add alcohol to the mix, and I become putty in her hands. Glazed over with love, my heart reaches out to her, to all her depths.

Every so often, I noticed the man from the bathroom staring at me. I couldn't tell if it was my lesbianism that intrigued him or if he wanted some of what he thought I'd taken, but I decided to take it as a compliment.

Esther and I danced and kissed in the crowded space. I inhaled the blend of her perfumes. She concocts her own scents and, each time, she smells slightly different, throwing a surprise party for my nostrils. This woman is a feast for all my senses. I thought to myself: I'd be okay if the whole world blew up right now, if this is how I go.

How silly, I answered myself. It's not blowing up and I'm not going anywhere. All I'm doing is holding this abundance wrapped in this tan, tiger-like body, close to me.

As we were kissing, I felt an annoying tap on my arm that was holding Esther's shoulder. I assumed it was a mistake caused by the crowd, where accidental friction is inevitable, but I felt it again, and then again. I broke away from Esther for a second and found myself face to face with Shelly, a Facebook friend I'd only seen through a screen for years.

"Hi!" I said to her, "What are you doing here?"

"I'm friends with Gidi," she answered.

She seemed a bit shocked by the dose of lesbianism she'd received straight to her face. For years, I had shared family pictures online. From the beginning of my relationship with Tom, then my eldest joined the photogenic sessions, followed by my middle daughter and, finally, my youngest son. One big happy family, the epitome of Facebook material.

"So you're..." Shelly tried to navigate her way to a question in this very obvious situation, but it seemed as though she'd made a wrong turn, couldn't find the words.

I helped her: "Esther is my beloved."

"How lovely," she gave the correct response, in a tone I could have interpreted, but chose instead to pretend I couldn't.

"Right. The loveliest," I said to her and turned my eyes away, back to the kiss waiting for me on Esther's lips.

Between social media and reality, sometimes you have to know what to choose.

# Touching the Same Path From Both Sides of Beauty

Our most erotic encounter didn't culminate in explosive climaxes or dazzling fireworks. It didn't even involve penetration. Instead, it was so gentle, its wildness so tightly leashed, that I remembered—or perhaps relearned—how the path to divinity can be delicate and unassuming. How the very air, in its intangibility, can strip us bare of our pretenses, and how sometimes the whisper of a finger is all it takes to cry out to the angels.

The most erotic sex began at a bar. "We're going out tonight," she declared. After a day of work, we slipped on jeans and jackets and ventured into the evening. No reservations, no set destination. We found ourselves at 'Samar Klasani' in Jaffa, perched at the bar. We shared two dishes of meat, delicate cuts from rugged pastures. We savored red wine, deeply Israeli in character—one glass for me, one for her. The bartender offered shots, but we declined. One glass of wine was precisely right, like a glove on a hand, like my hand on her thigh, like her thigh to exaltation.

Later, sated and eyes sparkling, we returned home and lay naked in bed. She reclined on her back, and I beside her. I began to caress her, my fingers tracing paths across her breasts, her stomach, her thighs. I gently explored every curve of one leg, then the other. My hand ghosted over her pussy, touching without touching, mostly not touching at all. I pressed close to her with gentle movements, on my side, facing her. My legs were closed, my hips swaying. I never stopped touching her.

The pleasure-seeking panther within her surrendered to my

touch as I continued on and on. I brushed her inner thighs, every part of her hips. With airy delicacy, I lightly grazed above her pussy, then returned to her legs, stomach, breasts. I revisited her groin, not touching her vagina, just skimming over and around it. I focused on her skin, her legs, her lower belly.

She lay on her back, legs parted, eyes closed. Occasional sounds of pleasure escaped her lips. I caressed every smooth expanse of her body. I touched every place I reached with love, from her knees to her neck. Without words, I loved all of her, letting her know that the world ceased to exist beyond her. I allowed passion to soften within me, to flow aimlessly through my being.

We could have continued like this for hours, and perhaps we did. We didn't check; time held no meaning. The only significance lay in the pleasure and the connection that had formed and was still forming, existing in those moments or hours or eternity of an evening. I cradled her thigh, her stomach. I was drawn to her as a teenage boy is drawn to a young woman (or so I imagine, having never been one). I was pulled towards her with an overflowing intensity, restrained by the boundaries of not-knowing. And perhaps that same not-knowing is what makes it free. I was a young man, I was a ripe woman, I was a coiling snake and I was a ruling queen. I knew nothing and I knew everything that mattered. My legs were closed, but I felt myself dripping, probably wetter than I'd ever been. I wanted her and I kept my desire restrained like a wild horse between my legs.

She floated inside the pleasure as one floats on the surface of water. She allowed my hands to roam over her, to dwell on every cell of her skin. She allowed her open pussy to feel me, almost without touch. She allowed my steady presence to be there, to gently stroke her desire like the wind caresses a face. I clung to her without wanting anything from her. I want everything from her in life. I poured myself into every crevice of hers that I could, because she is all that's right for me. Because her heart is the home I've searched for over many incarnations. Here, on this evening, with one glass of wine and open legs, I could let my desire to merge with her simply be.

The touching went on and on. Our bodies surrendered and softened, relaxed and condensed. Passion bubbled from between our legs and flowed between us like a wide, deep river. Our knees were its upright banks, round basalt rocks. We let it be, simply. We held it, rode it, until we didn't.

Our most erotic encounter ended with a few orgasms. We took them by demand, with a sudden clear desire. An explosion of "I want it," and they emerged from within us one after another, accompanied by deep moans like we know. Sometimes all you can do is climb the banks and let the river flood with nectar.

## He Has Something to Say

We pedal our bikes eastward down Eilat Street, headed to a meeting at a new printing house we want to try out.

Esther rides ahead of me. I love watching her against every backdrop—urban and sooty, desert-like, the lush green of Galilee, the blue lake. Against all colors this woman glows from within; how does she do it?

Her hair in a high ponytail, she pedals, her back ramrod straight. We form a line: two women, four legs, four wheels.

Cars stream by on our left. The single lane forces them to slow as they approach us, waiting for a chance to pass. When they do, they accelerate all at once, spewing exhaust into the street.

Electric bikes—mostly food delivery riders—buzz past us. Our bikes are the normal kind, old-school, and I feel my quads burning on the incline.

Eilat Street morphs into Jaffa Way, then into Menachem Begin Boulevard. We've turned east, still climbing. We pedal on.

The streetscape flows by: clothing shops, luggage stores with bags piled high. Graffiti adorns the walls—Band-Aids layered upon each other, a red heart, an alien swallowing a woman. On a peeling facade, someone has sprayed: "Without you, everything shakes."

The Levinsky market appears on our right. People move along the streets like blood through veins, seeping from openings, flowing onward. A vegetable stand displays price signs: oranges on sale, five shekels a kilo.

We press on to the sprawling LaGuardia interchange. Cars

veer right towards the tunnel while we halt at the pedestrian light, waiting for the traffic to thin.

The intersection teems with people. We're on the road, one foot on the curb, waiting with the crowd.

"Move to the right," a voice calls out. I keep my eyes fixed on the traffic light, waiting for it to change.

"Get up on the curb," I realize the voice is aimed at me and turn to locate its source. A tall man stands on the traffic island. Seeing he has my attention, he repeats, "Go ahead, get up, get up."

"Do you know me?" I ask him.

"What?" He's thrown off balance. I've pulled him out of context.

"Do you know me?" I repeat the question.

"No."

"Exactly," I reply.

It takes him a quarter-second of silence to grasp my meaning. Then he spits out, "I wouldn't want to know a bitch like you."

Oho. How quickly the ape emerges.

The light changes. Esther and I pedal forward, onward. We'll reach the printing house soon. The ape-induced stress clings to me for another hour.

## In the Beginning

*When you fuck me from behind,*
*Pumping me against (for) your body,*
*My mind escapes its skull and flies to the ceiling,*
*Scattering into pieces that float in circular movements above us.*

*When you fuck me from above,*
*Spirals explode from my clit to my belly,*
*Shivers splash across my nape,*
*Origami cranes take flight from my fevered shoulder*
*To distant lands.*

*When you grind against me, hip to hip,*
*I am grounded, melting into the mattress,*
*Creating craters of blazing pools.*
*I liquefy into the planet's core,*
*Fusing with magma beneath the ocean floor.*

*When we fuck,*
*All this happens at once,*
*And I think*
*I'm touching the secrets of creation*
*Within me.*

## I Do

*I know the depths of holiness,*
*The divine touch, the soft caress*
*To enter sanctity's embrace,*
*To find in it my rightful place*

*They cannot define what verse should be*
*Or bound the realm of femininity*
*Their rules of impurity fade*
*Before the beauty we have made*

*They cannot preach that blood is unclean,*
*When from my body, I convene*
*A silent cycle, nature's flow,*
*A rhythm only women know*

*They cannot mold love's form for me,*
*This comes from home, where I am free*
*God Herself, in all Her grace,*
*Resides within this sacred space*

# Deep and High, Exactly How I Like It

We kiss, and you ask me to undress you. "Strip yourself too," you command. I peel off your pants. No underwear—just how I like it. I shed my own clothes for you. What's for you is always for me too.

You fuck me with all your might, coming hard against me. Then again. And again. I'll never have my fill of you. I've waited years for this.

On my back, you lift my hips, my head pressing against the wall. You slide a pillow beneath me for comfort.

From the drawer of surprises, you pull out a dildo. "Don't move," you order, leaving to wash it quickly. I wait, legs splayed. "Stay still!" you shout from the bathroom.

I love it when you slip into commander mode. Returning, you kneel beside me, gliding the warm dildo over my clit. It feels warm, divine.

Slowly, you slide it inside. I swallow it hungrily, craving you so badly.

You fuck me relentlessly. One of my hands finds your warm cock, the other your pussy. Your breasts shimmer above me, a double gift of beauty.

It feels incredible. I'm about to burst with honey. You whisper golden lust, like you know how, words that fan the flames in my cunt.

Wild above me, you're in total control of your movements, your rhythm. I moan, climb, groan, then scream as I come on the dildo—your cock. My orgasm ignites yours, your yell chasing mine. A chain of grace weaves through the air, ascending higher and higher from the bed.

"All of Tel Aviv heard you," you grin.

"Good," I reply. "Maybe they'll learn something."

## Light Dragged Into the Heart of Darkness

*On the thirtieth day at your mother, Sarah's, memorial.*
*A grand piano stands in a crowded hall.*
*Men, lost in remembrance,*
*Speak of themselves.*
*Women, intertwined,*
*Speak of connections.*
*When Gabriel rises to play*
*A Brahms sonata,*
*You close your eyes*
*And weep.*

# Springtime on the Golan Heights

We entered the stream on a Wednesday morning. Everyone was in their routines, but we extricated ourselves from the city into nature, from dry land to water, to celebrate the holiday of your arrival in the world.

We drove down a rugged stone road until we reached a sign marking the trailhead. My little jeep is a ninja, unafraid of a few bumps. We left it resting in the shade beneath a tree, taking with us only two water bottles, a GoPro camera, and the car keys—which I secured to the top of my bathing suit for safekeeping.

You wore a bathing suit top and shorts; I, a bathing suit beneath my tank top and shorts. We both donned shoes, heeding the trail's clear warning: the path winds over rocks and river stones in the water—no flip-flops or bare feet allowed.

Willow and oleander trees formed a natural archway, and we passed beneath it ceremoniously. Cool water lapped at our ankles. The stream ran clear, revealing the slick, uneven rocks on the riverbed.

You walked ahead of me, your back a beautiful hue amidst the surrounding greenery. How does your skin manage to glow with both the warmth of the desert and the lushness of tangled vegetation? Even now, I'm in awe, though I should be accustomed to it after seeing your nakedness against so many landscapes.

Iridescent dragonflies darted around us, some metallic blue, others a deep burgundy. Nature's commotion pulsed around us.

The air was thick with the wild scents of almonds, figs, and mint. You detected the fig trees before they came into view. I recalled drinking whiskey and eating figs on our first date. The memory of how you watched me as I put the fig in my mouth remains indelible.

We moved with deliberate slowness, each step mindful. The rocks beneath our feet varied in size, slippery and sometimes coated with moss. We slowed down to a pace far removed from the city we'd left behind. River flora enclosed us, accompanied by a chorus of birds, insects, and toads.

The water was cold, the sun above offered its warmth. We paused occasionally to kiss.

You shed your bathing suit top, walking bare-breasted through the water. Your strong back teased me the entire way. Pink oleanders peeked at us from the riverbanks. Dragonflies had been our constant companions throughout the journey. I spotted two of them coupled on a branch. "Look, dragonflies fucking!" I called out to you.

You found yourself a stick to aid your navigation between the rocks, and I followed suit. We looked like three-legged crabs.

On the bank, among the reeds, a marsh turtle inched slowly into the water and vanished. You stripped off your shorts as well, now naked save for the shoes protecting your feet. You pointed skyward: "A crane on a cane," you said. Metallic blue and purple-red continued to swirl around us in a frenzy of beating wings.

Suddenly, you cried out, "Blackberries!" upon spotting an enormous tree laden with thousands of purple fruits, bursting with juice.

We reached into the tangled branches, plucking the ripest berries and feeding them to each other. Our hands and tongues stained purple. You shook the branches while I gathered the fruit that fell, floating gently downstream. We had become hunter-gatherers of sweet-tart delights.

We gorged ourselves like little monkeys until you declared

you'd had enough sugar. "It's not enough for me," I told you, settling down to harvest berries from the lowest branches that dipped into the water.

We pressed on, you naked and me trailing behind. Occasionally, tilapia fish swam alongside us. I spotted another pair of coupled dragonflies, then another, and another. "Look, two pairs right next to each other," I pointed out on a nearby branch.

We perched on rocks in the water to watch them—a live dragonfly porn show.

They flew through the air, joined together. Two by two. Couples and more couples connected on leaves, in flight, coupled on the earthen banks of the river.

As we continued, we gathered berries that had floated downstream, collecting them in hidden pockets between the rocks. We plucked them from the water and popped them directly into our mouths.

We ventured further along the river until the water deepened into cold lagoons. The bottom was no longer within reach. We swam and floated on our backs, faces to the sun, our bodies now accustomed to the cold water. White and orange butterflies fluttered nearby. The dragonflies persisted in their dance, alternating between circling and resting around us. They arrived solo or in pairs, flaunting their electrifying wing orgy.

Upon reaching a spot where we could stand, I spied a mulberry tree. The water reached our chests. We paused beneath the interwoven leaves and picked the fruit. The slightest touch sent them tumbling into our hands. We kissed with sweetened tongues.

The slickness of our tongues melded with the slipperiness of your naked body in the water. The sugar and your breasts pressed against me left me dizzy. You slipped your hand beneath my bathing suit and fucked me under the mulberry tree. Your gaze was hot and focused, like an extension of the sun. I came, squirting in the water. We kept moving. My heart raced as I half-walked, half-swam forward.

The water gradually receded to walking depth. First to hip level, then to our knees. I paused to capture a photo of dragonflies while you waited, perched naked on a round rock in the middle of the river. You squirmed on its surface and, as I drew near, you exposed your pussy to me. I sat in the water at your feet and licked your clit, your lips.

The cool rock chilled your inner thighs. The taste of your pussy mingled with the lingering flavor of berries in my mouth.

After three hours of walking in the water, we reached the river's exit and climbed onto dry land. The solid ground felt reassuring beneath our feet. We followed a white gravel path, surrounded by trees, bushes, and dry thorns.

Prickly plants with round inflorescences and stems covered in fine hairs stood erect among the thorns, dotting the yellowing thicket with splashes of purple.

# Everything Began When I Came to an End

We've cultivated a sweet tradition: on weekends with the kids, we cook for them or roll sushi together. On child-free weekends, we host parties at the studio or prepare celebratory dinners for friends. Today is Friday and, later, friends will be arriving at the studio for dinner.

This morning in bed, I was astride you. As I swayed, you whispered, "My wild one, I can feel your power."

You had propped a mirror against the sauna beside us, and now it reflected my body undulating atop yours in waves. "Gift me with your climax," you breathed. "I love it so much when you come."

Everything began when I came to an end. After my cry of ecstasy, when I was already thoroughly cooked, you flipped me over and worked your magic. You made me gush like the sea, transformed me into a fountain. You gently pounded my pussy with your fists from the outside, and I squirted more and more onto you. Only you know the depths of what I'm capable of.

Afterward, you turned me halfway, my hips facing you. We were inside each other, gazing at one another. We spoke in our secret language. I love you so much, Esther, I didn't know this was possible.

"Don't move inside me," you said, as you set the rhythm. "Fuck me like this," you said.

You flipped me over completely, unleashing your wild side in a frenzy of doggy-style passion. "Your ass is like two fresh buns," you said, then smacked them with your strong hands—once on the right cheek, once on the left. Your spanking was painful and precise, the kind that tenses your body and sharpens your intentions.

In a wave-like fuck, you came into me from behind and kept going. I climaxed from my ass; I don't understand how you do it, turning fiction into science. You came again and I mounted you, reaching another peak.

Finishing is certainly a phrase men gave to this thing that, for women, is just the beginning.

After countless climaxes that sparked even more climaxes, I'd say we were done and got out of bed, out of the studio, out of each other's bodies.

We ventured out to shop, cycling along paths the city had painted green, intoxicated by our many orgasms and our connection. I was in love with you like in the beginning, more than in the beginning—I always compare to the beginning. Maybe I should stop comparing, I mean, finish comparing, something that isn't like anything else.

We ate in the outdoor market, perched on low stools. The crowd hummed around us while my heart was as quiet as my pussy.

We bought flowers and bottles of wine, then returned to the studio to lounge in bed with newspapers, in our underwear.

I climbed on top of you again and came once more. "It's beyond my power," I told you.

"No, it's your power beyond measure," you answered with a smile. "Now let's go cook."

We go to the kitchen, where I assumed my usual role as your sous chef. You played Chopin on the speakers; a special quietude settles in my heart when you turn up the volume. While you tended to the fish, I sliced celery and peeled kohlrabi. I minced garlic cloves. You asked me to cut carrots. I began slicing them into circles, but you said, "Cut them in unexpected ways," and demonstrated.

Each knife strike on the carrot came from a different angle than the last, creating unusual shapes from this common vegetable. Only you, I thought, only you could cut it like this. Even the carrot didn't know it had such potential.

You roasted fennel and cherry tomatoes in one pan, peppers, carrots, and white sweet potatoes in another. In one skillet, you prepared Moroccan-style fish; in a second, Asian-inspired fish. Simultaneously, you cooked basmati rice, made a tangy radish salad, a cucumber and black sesame salad, and a green salad with goji berries.

Beside you, I chopped, peeled, and washed dishes. In less than an hour and a half you had dinner ready, the studio filled with comforting aromas.

When sweet-Gali, Nissan, Dominique, Shirley, and Michal arrived, we lit candles. We blessed the generosity of the creatress-of-all-that-exists and ate your world's-most-delicious food. We talked about art and gender, words and grace. We spoke of Elfriede Jelinek and Roxane Gay, and whether there is such a thing as bravery, or if sometimes there is no option but to dare. Between ignition and ignorance, between groping in the dark and knowing, sometimes a painting has no choice but to be painted, to realize itself in the act of creation, a tale has no choice but to be told.

You told us about Hilma af Klint, who explored the harmonic-mystical code of nature in her paintings, how she painted in an abstract style years before the 'fathers of abstract painting.' She requested that her paintings not be displayed for at least twenty years after her death and, in life, she refused to show or sell her work. We pondered: What is work? What constitutes that which we try again and again to touch? What is this intangible air from which we attempt to build poetry palaces for creation?

When we finished eating, we moved to the living room. You played the piano, and then Michal took over while you picked up the flute. I immersed myself in the permeable peals of notes you produced with the same ease as you had prepared the food. With the same soft touch you use to concoct your perfumes, with the same intelligent elegance you employ to create your paintings.

I'm learning from you about the aesthetics in every action, in every gesture. Nothing is too small for your attention, and nothing is bigger than your intention.

# It's a Disco

You're making the bed, piling pillows against the wall for our comfort. We undress. "Give me your hands," you say. I extend them, and you bind my wrists with a silver silk handkerchief.

You produce another handkerchief, this one black, and tie it over my eyes. My heart instantly begins to race.

"Lie down," you say, your tone half-telling, half-ordering. I recline onto the bed. "Lift your arms," you instruct, and I raise them above my head.

With my sight taken away, my other senses suddenly sharpen. You glide a cloth over my skin, igniting goosebumps atop a fiery sensation. Then comes the whip, its strips caressing me slowly, making my skin sing to you.

You straddle me. I feel your weight on my hips, our thighs embracing. It calms me to feel you close. The pressure of your body grounds me even as I soar higher under your whip's touch. You're merely teasing me with it, but the knowledge of its potential at any moment makes me tingle with excitement.

"Come," you say, leading me on a journey through darkness. You grasp the silver handkerchief between my hands, guiding me to the living room. There, you press me against the wall and lean in close. Our kiss is fiery. I lift my bound hands, cupping your breasts. You allow it. I'm your willing subject, your cheeky slave.

"On your knees," you command, and I sink down, discovering a pillow placed there for me.

You thrust your pussy into my mouth. Blind, I can only taste your exquisite flavor, your generosity. You fuck my mouth with fierce intensity, gripping the black handkerchief to control my head, drawing me closer to and farther from your pussy.

I never know if it's my mouth fucking your pussy or your pussy fucking my mouth. This time, shrouded in darkness, you're in complete command of your pleasure. It makes me wet, warm, and thick with desire.

"Come here," you suddenly demand, pulling me up to you. We kiss, and you taste yourself on my lips. You lead me back to the bedroom and order me to lie on my back.

"One second," you tell me, "Wait here, don't move." I sense you moving about, then you return and penetrate my aroused pussy.

You're fucking me with one of your dildos. You lift my feet to your shoulders, my legs straight, resting against you. I sense you're on your knees before me, pumping pleasure deep inside.

The air splits with a sharp crack, and I feel the whip on my thigh. I jolt, and you continue penetrating me with your cock. Another lash follows, then another, alternating between my thighs. Each strike is harder than the last. My thighs burn as you keep fucking me. The intensity builds, compressed and throbbing. You whip until my body jumps—I've reached my limit.

You reposition my feet back onto the mattress and lean in for a kiss. In the darkness, I feel you but can't anticipate your next move. It sends shivers through me, keeping me on edge.

You kiss me and whisper, "I'm learning you, learning exactly how much you'll allow me."

Resuming your thrusts, you massage my clit as you fuck me. I hear your passion mounting, your moans ascending. It feels overwhelming; my pussy wild with your intensity. I can no longer distinguish where you end and I begin. My only freedom lies in my pussy and my mouth. I hear myself cry out, "Esther, you're my hero!" You laugh with pleasure—I know the fifty shades of your voice, and none of them are grey. You fuck me even harder.

# The Repair in the Reflection

I lay prone as you sat astride my face, carrying yourself proudly above me. Facing the mirror, you gripped the bed railing as if it had been custom-built for upright lesbian fucking. Your hair was messy and wild, your breasts—the most beautiful in the universe—filled my view as I opened my eyes. You fed me your fresh, sweet, clever pussy. I was crazy wet. Thank goodness for the 'passionpad' beneath us.

I gushed all over myself as I devoured you. You fucked my mouth while I made myself squirt. I screamed and you silenced me with your cunt. You fucked my chin, pushing yourself inside me. I couldn't stop squirting.

I've long since stopped marveling at the source of these fluids, knowing I have no choice but to surrender. To squeeze and expel them, but not so hard as to scare them away. It's a delicate dance of pussy and consciousness, a balance between craving and knowledge.

"You're squirting on my back," you said. "More and more, you've got more, you naughty thing!"

Later we switched. You lay down and I sat upright, thrusting my pussy into your mouth. There's such healing in the mirror before us.

"Lie down here," you said, "and turn over."

You fucked me as I gazed into the mirror. Above, you were a lioness ascendant; below, I was your mirrored lion.

I surrendered with all my might, a formidable submissive. In that moment, you could have done anything to me, to any part of me, with any intensity.

This is absolute surrender, and there is no defeat in it.

You did with me as you wished, your desire is my desire.

It's like sitting in a bar and wordlessly calling you to come sit beside me. The power of feminine hypnosis, an advanced course in witchery.

Each of us draws abundance from this wishing well and, no matter how much we take, there is always more. The giving itself is the giver, let there be no confusion.

You came and made me moan. Your orgasm took a turn and ended up square, the kind that nourishes rather than drains. You came your orgasm inward to me or to yourself, I don't know if there's a difference.

I realized that silence can also be born from screams, and I remembered, again, that there are wisdoms only the body comprehends.

# Live Water

We restrained ourselves in the evening because of the children, and again in the morning for the same reason. We readied the little ones for camp, then headed to the beach with Michaela. While I rode the waves, you two ate watermelon on the shore. As you strolled along the sand, I hunted for the perfect swell. We waved at each other—you both from the beach, me from the sea.

Emerging from the water to you we kissed with longing; two hours is a long time for us to be in each other's presence without touching. Your body is the ultimate wave I crave.

Michaela watched us and laughed. "You're like teenagers," she said.

We reached the car, and I loaded the surfboard. I was still dripping wet. We were all in our swimsuits. A horny old man, eyeing the three women we are, blurted out his unsolicited and uninteresting opinion. "The beach is the best," he said. "So, you had fun, huh?"

The chasm between self-importance and lack of self-awareness collapses on the heads of old men, and they flounder there, as graceful as cockroaches in the trash room of a Tel Aviv apartment building. "Don't talk to us, shhh," you told him. He faltered, surprise at your response silencing his voice. After teaching the girl a lesson in assertiveness, we left.

We dropped off the big-little one at her father's and continued home. Our time finally caught up with us.

We stepped into the shower and immediately, without

hesitation, you slipped your hand inside me. After hours of anticipation, I was dripping wet for you. In the shower, under the stream, I squirted the sea we'd brought with us.

You clung to me and my longing began to quench. You directed the showerhead to your pussy. I knelt down to lick you. Water sprayed into my mouth. Hot water and hot pussy mingled on my face, spraying around and over me. Water on my cheeks, in my hair, in my eyes. Fireworks exploded in my cunt.

After you came in my mouth, you said, "Sit there." I sat before you on the floor, a good girl. I spread my legs and, with myself wide open in front of you, I watched you squirt all over me.

I stood and we fucked each other, the water fucking us both. We came again and again, one into the other.

On shaking legs, deconstructed and reconstructed, I stepped out of the shower. You followed. We got dressed and started our workday.

## Wisdom Arrives in its Entirety

We've entwined our bodies completely,
No zone is inaccessible
No skin is out of bounds.

The partial piece that is the body mingles
With the greater piece that is life.
The bones you gallop upon
Beg me to match your pace,
To fold away sorrow from space
To burn with you is to sign on to eternity.

We encapsulate moments of celestial presence
On the imagined timeline, existing only in flesh and bone.
The soul knows nothing of age,
Space knows not front from back
The body certainly does.

We craft a spaceship from our bed.
The blue bars support us when a hand needs
To grasp something with force,
To brace against the quaking of release.

Cradled shoulders pushed between moist lips
Sweat salts the forehead,
The collarbone, lapped up to the neck.
"God, what are you doing to me?" I ask.
"Whatever I want," you answer.

## As Much as Can be Held

Our time is almost spent. Soon I'll have to leave you. We slide into bed naked and begin to embrace. We kiss, gazing into each other's eyes, looking deep into happiness.

How did the world bring you to me? How did you come towards me in that packed bar and sit in the one empty spot, next to me? You came at exactly the right moment, when I was on the verge of breaking, when I had almost given in to compromise.

Your eyes sparkle with a blue that never ceases to mesmerize me. Your amber-toned skin is soft, warm, I can't help but glide over it with thirsty hands.

You place my hand on your beautiful cunt and I touch you with the delicacy of a dragonfly. I'm instantly wet. You're the weather goddess of my body, stirring the wind and bringing the rain.

Our eyes remain locked. I make love to your wise cunt with my fingers, and you whisper: "Your hands, the way you touch me."

You lay me on my back, enter my pussy and fuck me hard and steady. You say: "Did you think I'd let you go without making you squirt? Without fucking you?"

I'm already familiar with the tightening of my stomach, the stretching in anticipation and then the consent to relax and spray my cunt juices all over you. That intoxicating sensation of my fluids splashing over you and leaving large stains on the sheets.

The closeness I feel afterwards, the gratitude for the knots you've untied in me.

"Thank you for waiting for me," you said when you first sat down beside me.

"Yes, I was waiting for you," I replied, "Thank you for coming." And I didn't even know then how much.

You climb on top of me, fucking my thigh, my cunt wet and burning, our hips synchronized in a rhythmic pumping.

You're on me in a chain of orgasms that aren't really endings because they're unending. They're prefixes, they're ongoing present.

We turn onto our sides. I grip your hips as you rub against me and fuck me from behind. When I turn over completely, I'm already screaming, releasing more and more control and fluids. The depth you enter me, the depth revealed to me when you're behind me, it's a peak that keeps climbing. How you came to me at exactly the right time. How you keep coming.

All at once, you lie full-bodied on the bed and pull me on top of you.

"Do you want me to come a little?" I whisper to you, and you answer:

"Not a little. I want a lot. I want you to come hard, to give me this gift before you go." My mouth licks your neck, softly bites your shoulder. I'm so hot that a few movements on you are enough to make me come. Screams ascend like flames, warming the already steamy air around us.

You kiss my face and I kiss yours. Again your eyes are on me. Again that spark of yours that flies me to eternity. I was destined to love you. It was clear to me from the moment you first sat next to me, and I understand it more each time anew. I'm learning how to fly with you, with such a wide wingspan, a school for albatrosses could open on your sheets.

We step into the shower and with firm embraces you come on me again and again. My hands hold you and you can relax into me. I'll never leave. I will be with you even when I leave you soon. I waited a lifetime for you. I'll wait until the next time.

# ESTHER
# 2023

# The Upper Lesbelon

At Opa we caress food in ways we've never known. Charred cucumber strips embrace almond yogurt, nestling like a tender vulva in a potion of cucumber, rue, and wormwood's essence. We sit across from each other, eyes wide. She says, "What she does to food, this chef... that's what our sex does to my body."

Ten courses arrive in succession, each trembling our senses. Small in size, yet each one an effervescent universe unto itself. I close my eyes, placing a morsel of pickled melon peel with potato ice cream, chive, and dill on my tongue. This wild, unreasonable fusion brings tears to my eyes. I open them to find Esther across from me, her own eyes glistening. We exchange glances, "What is she doing to us?" we whisper, "How, for the love of fuck, will we ever eat anywhere else?"

Esther wears a silk suit adorned with drawings of monkeys fucking in various positions. Her hair is swept up in a high ponytail, black eyeliner framing her blue eyes. This woman... she is breathtaking.

She reaches across the table, and I caress the soft inner skin of her arm. "Are you still writing about our sex?" she asks.

"I'm done," I reply, "I don't need to anymore."

I was compelled to invent words for the indescribable. Once I found them, I could set them aside and revel in our sexuality primally, primordially. I no longer wish to unveil the ineffable to anyone else.

Her hands caress my skin—midwives to beauty birthed from God's cunt—sending ripples of excitement across my flesh.

Post-ganglionic neurons electrify my heart muscle. I may be seated in this restaurant but, in truth, I'm training for the Olympics of goosebumps. Esther's touch information travels through the brachial plexus. Like this food, my nerves reveal that the periphery, too, is the center.

"Your book will come out this year," she says, "I feel it in every fiber of my being."

Our gazes intertwine. I look at her, part of me believing, part of me yearning to believe. She says, "One of your eyes sees and the other is a mirror." As always, she's right.

We leave the restaurant in a daze, arms wrapped around each other's hips, still reeling from our experience. Wild, orange wine bubbles in our hearts. We've made plans to meet Daniella and Matan at a jazz bar, so we head there, laughing at the abundance of beauty in the city's ugly streets. Layers of black carbon have darkened the intersections. A lust for battles and property has folded the streets in on themselves. We wind our way upward, finding a rhythm of quiet among the cacophony of honking horns.

Perched on tall stools in a bar lined with records, we recount our culinary odyssey to Daniella and Matan. They immediately make reservations for themselves.

Our conversation meanders through the heart's choices, self-actualization, the layered nature of life, and the intricacies of unions. We speak of life-altering encounters, of the interplay between color and age. They are a sweet couple, a profound couple, and we delight in delighting with them.

The orange wine continues to flow as we drift homeward, frothing with joy. We lick each other's essential nutrients, acutely aware that no moment ever truly repeats. The food within us has transformed us, a reminder that we are never alone and, in one another, we will never be lacking.

Printed in Great Britain
by Amazon